LOVE'S MASQUERADE

Cassie Overton, sales director of her father's company, meets Alex Mayfield when he comes on business to strike a deal and they hit it off. Then Cassie is delighted to accept Alex's offer of a holiday, accompanying him back to his affluent family home in Tarango in the West Indies. Once there however, Cassie is compelled to comply with Alex's duplicity in fooling his grandfather and his brother Adam that she's his fiancée ... then finds it's Adam that she loves.

Books by Phyllis Mallett
in the Linford Romance Library:

LOVE IN PERIL
THE TURNING POINT

PHYLLIS MALLETT

LOVE'S MASQUERADE

Complete and Unabridged

LINFORD
Leicester

First published in Great Britain in 1989

First Linford Edition
published 2013

A catalogue record for this book is available
from the British Library.

ISBN 978–1–4448–1576–4

Published by
F. A. Thorpe (Publishing)
Anstey, Leicestershire

Set by Words & Graphics Ltd.
Anstey, Leicestershire
Printed and bound in Great Britain by
T. J. International Ltd., Padstow, Cornwall

This book is printed on acid-free paper

1

Cassie Overton grew more excited with every passing mile the airliner travelled, although she didn't betray her feelings to the man at her side.

She'd been excited by his suggestion back in London to take a month's holiday with him and, now they were nearing the West Indian island of Tarango, she was overwhelmed by the prospect of visiting a tropical paradise.

At first she'd refused to consider his offer, but Alex Mayfield was a handsome, persuasive man who had charmed her during the five months since she'd met him. Cassie had had time to get to know him pretty well and she knew that he would never do her any harm, which was why she had decided to accompany him. Now here she was, winging her way to Tarango with the exciting knowledge that she would spend four weeks in a whirl of sunny days and balmy nights.

She checked her reflection in her mirror, still dazed by the turn of events that had brought her this far. Her blue eyes glinted with excitement. It was not every day a girl found herself visiting a dream island with an attractive man who was also co-heir to a multi-million pound business.

She smiled as she recalled how they had met.

He'd come to her father's engineering company to the north of London, determined to get the best possible deal for his family business in the West Indies, and found that he'd to bargain with Cassie herself, a very shrewd sales director. They had hit it off from the start, and she'd come to enjoy his company.

He was an ideal companion, well educated, intelligent and amusing. There was a secret fiancée back home, he had told her, and what he needed while he was away was feminine company to stave off the great loneliness he felt.

Unattached herself, Cassie had respected his honesty in this matter and liked him well enough to accept his terms. When his European business ended, he'd offered her a month's holiday at his home on a beautiful island, and she'd happily accepted.

Alex was dozing at her side, and when she accidently nudged him he opened his dark eyes to look at her. She saw him smile as he checked his watch.

'Only another thirty minutes.' His eyes gleamed. 'We're almost home, and I can't wait to see Grandfather's face when I introduce you. It'll also be a big shock for Adam. He and Grandfather would like to see me settle down and pull my weight in the business, but I think there's plenty of time to get into harness. A man is only young once.'

'There is such a thing as responsibility,' Cassie reminded him, 'and if your twin brother has buckled down to his family duty then you ought to consider doing your share.'

'All I want at the moment is some money from the inheritance Grandfather Tobias holds in trust for me. I need to finance a business deal in Paris, then I can spend the rest of the summer in the Mediterranean.'

'Is that your prime reason for coming home?' Cassie's eyes were shrewd as she studied his handsome face. There had been no romance between them because of Kirsty, the girl he planned to marry some day, and he'd never indulged in anything other than a brotherly kiss.

'That's my only reason,' he replied with a smile, 'and I have to be careful how I broach the subject of money. If Grandfather doesn't think of a good reason why I shouldn't have it, then Adam surely will.'

'And where do I figure in all of this? I've been wondering why you asked me along. I had a feeling that there would be more to it than a straightforward holiday.' She regarded him with a serious expression, having late doubts now about accepting his invitation.

'It's not like that, honestly,' he assured her. 'There's nothing to worry about. Grandfather knows that I like to have myself a good time and that's why he's become cautious about giving me money over and above my allowance. Now I have to practically beg for what is rightfully mine. Half of Grandfather's estate will come to me when he dies, but he's a tough old man, and I want to live in my accustomed style until I do come into my inheritance,' he added frankly.

'You shouldn't talk like that!' Cassie was startled by his statement. 'I hope you're not planning something distasteful, Alex. I won't be a party to anything underhand. I made that quite clear before we left London.'

He chuckled. 'Look, you have nothing to worry about, I assure you. You will be very well accepted by my family, and you'll find it easy to charm Adam.'

'Why are you expecting me to charm

your brother?' Cassie's lips pulled into a firm line as she studied his face.

But he merely smiled and shook his head. 'I'm not! All you have to do is enjoy your holiday.'

'Then why bring me along if I don't have to play an active part in your plans?' Cassie asked, suspicion still lingering in her mind.

'I told you back in London that there are no strings attached,' Alex assured her again.

She studied his smooth face. He was tanned, with glinting brown eyes and thick, wavy brown hair. There was no doubt that this man was attractive and Cassie suspected that he'd use his looks and charm to get what he wanted out of life. She suppressed a sigh. Alex was a rogue but a charming one.

'I've gone along with your original proposal that we don't get romantically involved,' she told him, 'but I warn you that I won't be a party to any scheme you may have for extracting money from your family. I wish now that I

6

hadn't agreed to come with you,' she added, the pleasure and excitement she'd felt earlier now leaving her.

'Come on, Cassie, don't take that attitude,' he said. 'Your holiday was a perk thrown into the business dealings I had with your father's company, nothing more. I thought you'd like the idea.' He placed a hand on her arm. 'Adam will check you out very closely, I shouldn't wonder.'

'Your brother.' Cassie frowned. 'If what you've told me about him is true then it's a pity you're not more like him.'

'Adam is all right but he takes life far too seriously. He's always maintained that every daylight hour was made for working.'

'While you think that every hour, day or night, is made for pleasure!'

He shrugged. 'Life was meant to be enjoyed. You don't have to keep your nose to the grindstone all the time. Don't get too uptight about this visit, Cassie. Just relax and enjoy yourself.'

'So long as that's the only reason you invited me to your home,' she warned, looking younger than her twenty-two years. Fair-haired, and with appealing blue eyes, her face was small and heart-shaped.

Cassie's success in her father's business was due to the fact that she was clever, forthright, and down-to-earth.

Alex smiled. She knew he was genuinely fond of her even if he would use her to get what he wanted. At twenty-nine, Alex was well set in his ways, and Cassie was wise enough to know that nothing could change him. Any girl who fell in love with him would have to like his way of life because he would go on doing his own thing until the day he died.

She couldn't help wondering about his motives as she relaxed in her seat. When she looked at him, trying to read something from his expression, he grimaced mockingly, and she smiled and shook her head. He was so carefree that she couldn't help but find his manner infectious.

After landing and passing through Customs, Alex superintended the collection of their luggage. He escorted her to a taxi and she sank into the rich upholstery as he gave instructions to the driver. Her pulses quickened when the taxi took them through a small town clustered on the slopes of a mountain.

The buildings surrounded a tiny natural harbour, and after passing through the town, they followed a winding, dusty road that led into the interior of the island.

Looking back through the rear window, Cassie saw the harbour and the town far below, and to the right the rugged coast stretched away in a convex curve, the brilliant blue of the sea fringed with palm trees and silver sand. The scene looked like something out of a travel brochure, and she gazed at it in wonder.

'It was worth bringing you along just

to see the expression on your face,' Alex remarked, glancing at her. 'All of this is too familiar to my eyes, and it takes someone like you, who really appreciates it, to bring home to me just what I have here.'

'It's fabulous!' Cassie looked to her left, where the mountain ranged upward in desolate sweeps. The sky was perfectly blue.

Birds of brightly coloured plumage were darting hither and thither, busy about their natural tasks under the densely foliaged trees that lined the road. There was a profusion of flowers, too, of all bright hues and shades, and she drank in the scenery avidly.

'I need to be in the south of France in a month's time,' Alex said suddenly.

'Won't you have to explain this business venture you're hoping to finance?' she queried.

'I have some facts and figures to show Grandfather, but if I know Adam he'll veto my plans out of hand.'

'Why should he do that if it's a good

business venture?'

'Because he thinks my ideas are no good!' He spoke ruefully. 'Adam's like that. Just because he's Grandfather's right-hand man he thinks he's the only one who can handle the business. I never had the opportunity to show what I can do.'

'Because you've always shown a preference for personal indulgence?' She raised a shapely eyebrow. 'Poor Alex. Nobody understands you, I'll bet.'

'Don't mock!' He chuckled, and as the car swung round a tight bend in the road he was thrown against her. He slid an arm around her shoulders and kissed her lightly on the forehead. 'I think, in the five months since we met, you've come to know me better than anyone else in the world.'

'You said something about your parents dying at sea, didn't you?' She leaned against him for a moment.

'They disappeared in the Bermuda Triangle about twelve years ago,' he told her. 'Their yacht was never seen

11

again; not so much as a piece of wreckage. Grandfather brought us up after the tragedy, but it's not the same as having your own parents.'

He fell silent, and Cassie left him to his thoughts. She gazed from a side window, watching the exotic scenery flashing by.

When the taxi turned off the main road and followed a rutted access road through clumps of wild flowers and green shrubbery, Alex sat up a little straighter and glanced around.

'Cassie,' he said, leaning forward, 'just watch through the windscreen and you'll get your first glimpse of the place I call home. I haven't seen it very often in the past five years, but it still has the power to wring some emotion from me.'

Cassie leaned forward and saw a dull red roof showing amidst tall trees of several different shades of green. They passed under the trees and stopped at the bottom of a flight of stone steps that led up to a terrace fronting a great, white-painted house. Large windows studded the face of the building.

There were masses of flowers on the terrace, in urns and hanging baskets, their combined scent quite overpowering as Alex alighted and turned to take hold of Cassie's arm, to help her out of the car.

'Welcome to Mayfield Grove,' he said, suddenly serious despite the smile on his lips. 'I hope you'll enjoy your stay here, Cassie.'

'Masta Alex, what in tarnation are you doing standing out there in the heat?' A penetrating voice cut through the silence that enveloped them, and Cassie saw a massive dark-skinned woman approaching from the open front entrance.

There was a wide smile upon her dusky features which belied the stern note in her voice. She paused as Alex with his hand still holding Cassie's arm, began to ascend the steps towards her.

'Martha! It's good to see you again.' He kissed the housekeeper's broad, shiny black face. 'How's Grandfather? I'm afraid I haven't been in touch as often as I ought to have done, but I didn't think anyone would miss me.'

'Now, Masta Alex, you know you shouldn't talk like that.' There was a friendly smile on Martha's face despite the mild reproof in her voice. 'Some-one's got to do the work around here if you won't.'

'Where is everyone?' Alex glanced around, and Cassie noticed that he wasn't quite as confident as he would have liked her to believe.

'Masta Adam's at the mill. They been havin' bother there for a while.'

'What kind of bother? Are the workers on strike for more money?'

'You know nobody would kick against the conditions they got right here!' she replied, looking at him in exasperation.

'It's something to do with the new machinery they put in,' she added, mollified by his repentant expression.

'So Adam is in the thick of it as

usual,' Alex said. 'Where's Grandfather?'

'He ain't been so good lately. I say he's been overdoing it but he won't hear of it, naturally. The doctor told him to start taking things easy, but you know your grandfather. If he don't put in a ten-hour day then he thinks he's slacking.'

'Is it anything serious?' There was concern in Alex's voice.

'What can you expect with a man of seventy?' Martha shook her head. 'What can you expect when he's told to take it easy because his whole body's wearing out but he ignores the advice?' She tut-tutted. 'I've been doin' the best I can but it's got so a body can't do right no matter what she tries. I sure hope you've come home to stay longer than your last visit.'

'Yes. Well, we'll have to see about that.' Alex glanced at Cassie and smiled. 'Martha, I want you to meet Cassie Overton.'

Martha turned her attention to

Cassie and her face immediately changed expression. 'Miss Cassie,' she said in a honeyed tone, holding out a large hand while her face creased into a broad smile. 'I'm sure pleased to meet you, and if I'd been told in advance that you was comin' I would have had a room made ready for you. But it won't take me two shakes of a lamb's tail to get the place right.'

'Go on with you, Martha!' Alex teased her. 'Every spare room in the house is always ready for guests. Where's Grandfather?'

'In his study, goin' over the accounts, most likely. There ain't much that escapes his eyes, as you rightly know. You better let him know you're home.'

'Come on.' Alex held out a hand to Cassie and she grasped it. 'Let's go and introduce you to Tobias, the head of the Mayfield family. And don't worry about the kind of reception you might get. These days, Grandfather's bark is worse than his bite.'

He led her into the house, and

Martha disappeared through a doorway beyond the wide staircase that occupied the right-hand side of the large wall. There was an ornate chandelier hanging over the foot of the stairs, and a beam of sunlight striking through a window caused a brilliant starburst to explode in the heart of it.

The hall was surprisingly austere, the wooden floor highly polished and smelling of beeswax. There were some small rush mats here and there, and coolness seemed to be the keynote after the heat outside. The walls were colour-washed a delicate ivory and paintings adorned them. Several cane chairs set at strategic positions were the only furniture.

A number of closed doors leading off the hall broke up the smooth continuity of the walls, and Alex led Cassie toward one of them. He paused and looked into her face, holding her shoulders tightly as he commanded her attention.

'Listen to me before we go in, Cassie,' he said in a suddenly urgent voice. 'You heard what Martha said about Grandfather's health. It's probably only old age but we can't be too careful. He mustn't have any shocks or unpleasant surprises, so whatever I say to him about us, just play along with it.'

'What do you mean?'

He didn't take time to answer her question. Instead he thrust open the door, and conducted her into the room, where she saw a white-haired man sitting behind a large desk.

Cassie caught her breath as he looked up, disturbed by their entrance. When he saw Alex, his expression of annoyance was replaced by a smile. He started to rise, then appeared to change his mind and he remained seated.

Cassie was propelled forward, feeling distinctly uneasy at what Alex had said.

'Grandfather, how are you?' Alex moved around the desk until he was standing at the older man's side. 'Still hard at work?' he put a hand on Tobias's shoulder, and Cassie fancied that his flippant tone was masking his real feelings.

'Alex, my boy.' Tobias had a large, open face that was heavily wrinkled. His eyebrows and thick moustache were white. Grey hair had receded from the front and the top of his head and his skin was tanned to a rich shade of old mahogany by many years of living in the tropics.

Cassie remained in front of the desk, watching closely. She saw Tobias look up at Alex, smiling happily, and she was touched by the emotion which seemed to pervade the big room. She had believed from what Alex had said about his family, that his brother and grandfather were linked in opposition against him. Now, however, she could see real pleasure in the older man's expression as he greeted his grandson.

'Grandfather, before I launch into an account of my past six months, let me introduce you to Cassie. Cassie, this is my grandfather, Tobias Mayfield. Grandfather — Cassie. I wrote that she and I are contemplating marriage, and now I'm delighted to tell you that there should be a wedding within the year.'

Cassie was moving around the desk to the older man's side when the import of Alex's words reached her. She paused and stared at Alex, who was smiling easily but with tension showing in his dark gaze.

He frowned, willing her to continue as if he had spoken the truth, then glanced pointedly at his grandfather, who was smiling at her.

'Cassie, my dear, welcome home. I hope you will be very happy here. Alex did write about you, and I must say that his description has not done you full justice, but then he isn't a poet.'

Tobias held out a thin hand that trembled slightly, and Cassie forced a smile as she clasped his gnarled fingers. Her mind was in turmoil, although she managed to keep her voice steady when she replied.

'You're very kind, Mr Mayfield. I've heard so much about your home, and

Alex has told me a lot about his family.'

'Then you must have heard some very odd stories!' Tobias chuckled. 'Alex has a peculiar outlook on life.'

Alex laughed but there was a tenseness about him and he was obviously anxious to control the conversation. He moved around Tobias's chair and put a hand on Cassie's shoulder, squeezing hard with his fingers, warning her to play along with whatever he said.

Cassie fumed inwardly, aware that she couldn't deny anything in case she upset Tobias, who looked frail and weak despite the appearance of strength he evinced.

'Grandfather, you know my heart is in the right place,' Alex said, with forced lightness. 'Now that I have Cassie I'm planning to settle down. I haven't wasted my time while seeing the sights of Europe. There are some business leads I want to pursue, but all that can wait until I've been home for a few days.'

'How long do you plan to stay this time?' Tobias leaned his elbows on the desk and rested his chin in his cupped hands. He smiled at Cassie and, as Alex skated around the question, he interruped his grandson. 'Please forgive me for not rising to greet you, Cassie,' he apologised. 'My strength is almost exhausted. I feel the heat a great deal these days, so I must crave your indulgence.'

'Then we'll leave you in peace,' Alex said quickly. 'Come on, Cassie, let's get settled in then I can start showing you around. I've told you so much about the place that you must be dying to see it.'

'Yes, please make yourself at home, Cassie,' Tobias said, warmly. 'There will be time enough later for us to get acquainted. You'll soon meet Alex's brother Adam, who has been impatiently awaiting your arrival.'

'That sounds ominous.' Alex frowned. 'I hope you and Adam haven't been putting your heads together over this new development in my life, Grandfather. I assure you that I am in deadly earnest. I brought Cassie home to finalise our wedding plans.'

'Forgive me for asking,' Tobias said gravely. 'But your sudden intention to marry isn't based on the fact that two hundred thousand pounds will automatically be paid into your bank account upon the event of your marriage, is it?'

'Grandfather!' Alex simulated shock while he gazed frowningly at Cassie, his expression warning her to remain silent.

'I'm sure Cassie will excuse my attitude,' Tobias continued gently. 'I cannot be too careful, Alex, especially after some of the ploys you have used in the past to get money from your Trust.'

'I was young then, and foolish!' Alex's expression was taut despite his light-hearted tone. 'But all that is behind me. I am going to settle down, and I'll need all the help I can get.'

'If you are serious about that then you'll get all available help without having to ask for it,' Tobias assured him readily. 'It's about time you began to justify your existence. I really thought you'd never grow out of your boyish ways. This is good news, Alex. Just what the doctor ordered, in fact. Now, install Cassie in the best guest-room. She and I will get together later. I have to go up to my room to rest.

'Make yourself at home, Cassie,' he said again, 'and we'll spare no effort to make your stay a happy one. Are you aware that your father and I are old friends?'

'I didn't know that.' Cassie glanced at Alex, who nodded. 'I shall be happy to talk to you later, Tobias, and thank you. I'm sure I'll enjoy my holiday.' She smiled and turned to leave, and was pushed firmly from behind by Alex, who was intent upon getting out of his grandfather's presence before anything more could be said. When she turned in the hall to face him he held up a warning hand.

'I know, I know,' he said. 'But don't

say anything. Just think of Grandfather's health. We can't afford to upset him.'

Before Cassie could think of a reply, a keen voice cut in from behind her.

'Well, well, so you're back, Alex! Run short of money again? What scheme have you got in mind this time?'

'Adam!' Alex went forward with outstretched hand to the man who had entered the hall from outside. 'I'm glad to see you! How have you been keeping? Martha tells me you're working as hard as ever.'

'Hello, Alex.' Adam Mayfield shook hands warmly with his twin brother, and Cassie stared at them with mounting interest. 'I want to warn you before we go any further that Grandfather isn't very well, and certainly not up to trying to cope with your usual run of schemes. Give him a chance this time and you'll have my blessing to stay as long as you wish.'

'Don't worry about it.' Alex grinned at Cassie. 'I want you to meet the woman I plan to marry, Adam. This is Cassie. I wrote to Grandfather about her. Cassie, this is my twin brother, Adam. You can see the family resemblance,' he added.

She murmured a greeting, keenly aware of the sharp scrutiny to which she was subjected by the most discerning brown eyes she had ever seen. The likeness between the two men was uncanny, even his voice sounded exactly the same as Alex's. But his manner was different.

He was decisive and correct where Alex was casual and carefree. He held Cassie's gaze while extending his hand in greeting and, when she took hold of it, he gripped with powerful fingers.

'How do you do, Cassie?' He looked searchingly into her face. 'Welcome to Mayfield Grove. I hope you will enjoy your stay here.'

'Thank you, Adam.' She removed her hand from his a little nervously. He was obviously more serious-minded than Alex, but there was something about him which warned that he could be an implacable enemy if circumstances decreed, and she sensed hostility in him, which added to her uneasiness.

'I read the letter you wrote to Grandfather, and you sang Cassie's praises quite highly,' Adam observed, glancing at Alex although his attention was firmly upon Cassie. 'I understand that you're William Overton's daughter, and you met Alex when he did business with your father's company. What exactly do you do for a living, Cassie?'

'I'm the Sales Director of Overton Engineering,' she responded.

'And if you're thinking that she got the job because her father is the boss and it's her pretty face alone that sells Overton's wares then forget it,' Alex interpolated, grinning at Cassie. 'She's a tough business-woman, Adam, which is one of the reasons why I formed a relationship with her. I've been impatient to get her here to see how you measure up against her. You fancy yourself as the whizz kid of all Tarango but I'd bet on Cassie against you any day. She had me practically tearing my hair out more than once during our negotiations, I can tell you.'

'Then she's different from the type of woman you usually get to know!' Adam responded, and his cynical smile indicated that privately he thought otherwise.

Cassie caught her breath, her mind still reeling from the shock of Alex's lie to his grandfather. This all seemed like a bad dream. Why had Alex told that lie about their relationship? And what about his secret fiancée on the island?

She'd only arrived on this island a short time ago and already Cassie was having regrets about accepting Alex's invitation.

2

'Let's go into the library,' Adam suggested. 'I could do with a drink.' His gaze remained on Cassie as he crossed the hall and opened another door.

Alex led the way into the library and Cassie followed, having to brush past Adam, who waited for her to precede him.

Alex asked Cassie what she wanted to drink.

'Just a sherry,' she replied nervously.

Alex walked to the big cabinet standing near the window, poured a drink and brought it to Cassie.

He looked at Adam, who had moved to stand with his back to the impressive brick fireplace.

Cassie was only too aware of Adam's presence despite the fact that she pretended to be interested in the book-lined walls.

'What will you have, Adam?' Alex asked.

'Whisky and soda, please.' Adam smiled at Cassie, who was finding it difficult not to stare at him. 'What kind of a trip did you have?'

'Uneventful.' Alex answered as he poured two whiskies and splashed them with soda. He took one to Adam before moving to Cassie's side, where he drank some of his whisky.

Cassie realised he was far more nervous in his brother's presence than he'd been while they were with Tobias.

She was still feeling ill at ease herself, and Adam's intent gaze made her more nervous. Her excitement had been forced into the background by Alex's statement of their intending marriage, and she would never forgive him for creating such a situation.

She met Adam's gaze and was disconcerted a little to see him smiling. His very expression seemed to indicate that he was aware of the undercurrents seething in her mind. His dark gaze sliced through her defences and the fact that he looked so much like Alex added to her sense of confusion.

But there were differences of personality between them and, as she studied him, Cassie felt that he was more like the man she felt Alex should be. He was purposeful, determined, and had maturity and confidence, which Alex seemed to lack or conceal. The fact that he spent much of his time working hard on the estate had moulded Adam into a more compact figure. His movements were more studied, and there was a hint of latent power about him which added to his masculinity.

'Congratulations,' Adam said, interrupting her flow of thoughts. 'I have always said that the best thing which could happen to you, Alex, is a good wife.' His dark gaze swept Cassie again as he raised his glass, and she was startled to see his cynical expression.

'Mind you,' he continued, 'if you go about your future with as much care as you handled your past, Alex, then you're in for a rough time, and that applies also to any woman rash enough to marry you. But it goes without saying that I'll do what I can to help, so long as you don't do anything to hurt Grandfather.'

'There's no need to put on the big brother act,' Alex retorted. 'I care as much about Grandfather as you.'

'I've never doubted that, although at times you've had a strange way of showing it. But he isn't up to receiving shocks now. That much has changed since you were last home. He may not look it, for you know he always puts on a tough image, but he's frail inside. Time has caught up with him. So heed my warning, Alex.'

In the silence which followed this there was a knock at the door, and Martha entered carrying a large tray which she placed on a side table close to Adam's left elbow.

Martha gave them coffee before departing quietly. The silence that ensued then seemed even more loaded with tension. Cassie glanced at Alex to see that he was staring out at the mountain, the fingers of his right hand tapping impatiently upon his knee.

'How long have you two known each other?' Adam asked then.

'Five months.' Alex spoke before Cassie could even frame the words. 'And I've enjoyed every moment of her company. She taught me a great deal about business methods. You must remember what a hard time I had trying to clinch that series of deals with Overton Engineering. Well, that was all due to Cassie's acumen.'

Adam nodded. 'I must admit that there was some tough bargaining, and you handled that side of the business extremely well, Alex.' There was a grudging tone in his voice. 'Your efforts had a bonus attached,' he added, looking at Cassie. 'But now you're home,' he continued, 'and you'll have to start pulling your weight around here. Since Grandfather has been ill I've had to handle most of his work in addition to my own, and it's too much for one man.'

'We'll discuss it later,' Alex told him quickly. 'What about you while I've been away, Adam? Have you made any plans for marriage?'

'To Simone, do you mean?' Adam smiled and shook his head. 'No, I'm still looking for the perfect woman.'

'I always thought you would marry before me,' Alex said then. He caught Cassie's look of disapproval and narrowed his eyes at her warningly, causing her to sigh in exasperation.

'Is something wrong, Cassie?' Adam demanded instantly. 'You seem upset about something.'

'Sorry.' She was startled by his perception and hastened to conceal her feelings as she met his compelling gaze. 'It's just that I'm exhausted after our long trip.' The excuse came readily to her lips, and she lowered her gaze.

'Of course!' Adam arose, his face registering concern. 'Please forgive me,' he said easily. 'I'm so thoughtless, and I can see that you are showing signs of jet lag. Alex, show Cassie up to her room. I think Martha is putting her into the big one overlooking the bay.'

Alex stood up, unable to conceal his relief. 'Come on, Cassie, you can chat to Adam later. He'll probably want to interrogate you. He's always been suspicious of anyone I've ever shown an interest in, and he's probably thinking right now that it's the Mayfield millions you're after.' He smiled. 'But I'll tell you something. Mayfield money is very difficult to get hold of, even if one is entitled to some of it.'

Adam smiled too. He came across to take hold of Cassie's hands as she arose. 'Pay no heed to Alex,' he advised. 'He has such a warped sense of humour! I'll wager he's told you that Grandfather and I wouldn't welcome anyone he brings home. He thinks we are rather behind the times, preferring to remain here and run the business to gallivanting around the world as he does. But I assure you that I, at least, am very interested in whom my twin brother decides to marry, and I shall want to get to know you well in the time you are planning to stay.'

'Cassie will be here for about a month,' Alex said, pointedly.

'Have you set a date for the wedding?' Adam changed the subject so abruptly that Cassie couldn't respond.

But Alex merely smiled and shook his head. 'We're home so that Cassie can find out what life is like on the island. We'll probably come to a decision during the holiday. More than that we cannot say at the moment.'

'That's all right. There's no need for haste, is there?' Adam's eyes were bleak despite his smile, and Cassie caught her breath. He was still holding her hands, she realised, and withdrew them quickly and turned away.

Alex was standing by the opened door. Cassie walked towards him, head held high, but there was a tingling sensation along her spine. She sensed that Adam knew exactly what was going on, and he probably believed that she was as bad as Alex in that she had agreed to help him with whatever scheme had been concocted to get more money out of the estate.

She left the library with a sense of relief, aware that she ought to insist upon Alex telling his brother the truth about their relationship.

She turned to Alex when they reached the foot of the stairs, but he placed a finger against his lips, cautioning silence. She glanced past him and saw Adam standing in the doorway of the library, watching them intently.

Heaving a sigh, Cassie turned on her heel to ascend the stairs and Alex mounted at her side, attempting to hold her arm, but she pulled away from him, and when they reached the top, Martha emerged from a bedroom, her dusky face beaming.

'This is your room, Miss Cassie,' the housekeeper said. 'It's light and airy. I'm sure you'll love it. I always think it's the best room in the house.'

'Thank you, Martha.' Cassie entered the room and paused on the threshold to look around. Pale green was the dominant shade in the colour scheme. She noted the whitewood furniture, the three-quarter size bed, and immediately fell in love with the room. 'This is beautiful!' she exclaimed.

'You like it?' Martha was pleased, and moved to a door and opened it. 'Here's the bathroom. It has everything you might need.'

'Thank you.' Cassie spoke enthusiastically. She glanced at Alex, who was lounging in the doorway. 'I don't know why you spend most of your time wandering around the world when you have a home like this,' she told him.

'Some people are never satisfied with what they have,' he told her with a shrug. 'I expect that I am one of them.'

Martha spoke then. 'If there is anything you should need, Miss Cassie, please don't hesitate to ask for it.'

'Thank you, Martha.' Cassie smiled,

but, when the woman departed, her smile faded. She confronted Alex sternly. 'How could you do this? It was too bad of you,' she told him. 'You know your grandfather isn't well and yet you've lied to him about us! I don't see any reason why you should have done that, and as soon as I get the opportunity I'm going to set Adam straight about this situation. He's already looking at me as if I were a gold-digger!'

Alex smiled. 'Adam would be suspicious,' he retorted. 'Someone has to keep an eye on the Mayfield fortune. But don't be too hasty in your desire to set matters right. If you tell Adam anything now I won't get a penny of what is rightfully mine.'

'I refuse to be a party to your duplicity! I mean it, Alex. Either you explain to Adam or I shall tell him.'

'Don't be silly!' He sighed. 'I need funds urgently. You know that I wouldn't resort to this kind of subterfuge if I were not desperate. And we're not doing anything criminal. It is my money!'

'I wish you hadn't brought me along!' Cassie protested. 'I have a feeling that I'm not going to enjoy this holiday one iota.'

'Nonsense! You'll forget everything when you start acting the tourist. Now, why don't you have a shower and afterwards you could lie down and have a nap? We can talk again later.'

'Later will be too late to change your story to Adam,' she told him sternly.

'I don't plan to.' There was a stubborn set to his chin. 'He might be my twin brother but he's worse than Grandfather where money is concerned.' He turned away. 'Get some rest and I'll see you later, Cassie. I'm going to have to chat with Adam, make some kind of an accounting to him, and I need to get my story right.'

He departed, and Cassie went to inspect the bathroom and turn on the shower. After undressing, she stood under the streaming jets of water and let them caress her skin. Tension fled from her mind as she relaxed. Later, she dried herself and dressed casually in slacks and a red cotton suntop.

The journey and all that had happened since had tired her and the bed looked inviting. She lay down on it with a sigh of relief.

Closing her eyes, she drifted into slumber, and knew nothing more until a sound cut through her sleep and disturbed her. Half rising, and expecting to see Martha or Alex, she was surprised by the sight of a dark-haired elegant woman standing in the room regarding her.

'I'm sorry! Did I wake you?' There was an attractive accent in the woman's voice which Cassie couldn't immediately recognise. 'I'm looking for Adam.'

'Why should you think he might be here?' Cassie asked, puzzled despite the fact she wasn't quite awake.

'It was his mother's room, and sometimes he sleeps here,' the woman told her.

'Well, he won't be using it for the next month!' Cassie tried to remember the name of the woman Adam had been linked with.

'You're Cassie, I presume.' The woman came to the foot of the bed, her dark eyes gleaming. She was aged about thirty, Cassie judged. 'I heard that you had arrived,' she continued, 'and that you and Alex are planning to get married. I'm Simone Marchant. Perhaps Alex told you about me?'

'Yes, he did.'

Alex's lie was apparently having repercussions all around the island, Cassie realised. 'Forgive me,' she added, 'I was sleeping off the effects of my journey.'

'I am the one who should apologise,' Simone told her, but made no move to go. 'So you are staying for a month,' she said then. 'When are you and Alex getting married?'

'We haven't set the date yet.' Cassie felt fresh anger towards Alex for involving her in this unpleasant situation. She slid her feet off the bed and stood up to find that she was slightly taller than Simone.

Cassie sensed an underlying hostility in the woman and wondered why everyone seemed to be against Alex. There had to be more to it than the fact that he had allowed his twin brother to do all the work around the place while he lived it up in the pleasure spots of the world.

'Do you like Tarango?' Simone inquired.

'I like what I've seen so far. You live on the island?'

'I have for twelve years. My father owns the neighbouring estate.' Simone turned to the door, where she paused. 'I hope you will enjoy your holiday,' she said, and there was a hard expression upon her face. She made a motion with her hands. 'But there is one thing you should understand from the outset. Adam is mine!' Her glance cut at Cassie. 'He doesn't know it yet but he is going to marry me!'

'I came here with Alex,' Cassie protested mildly. 'I have no interest in Adam.'

'You wouldn't be the first girl who came here with Alex but made a play for Adam.' Simone's eyes narrowed as they held Cassie's gaze. 'So I'm warning you!' She turned abruptly and departed.

Cassie listened to her receding footsteps for a moment then walked to the door and watched her descending the stairs. She was shocked by Simone's attitude and, thinking of Alex, of the trouble he was certainly stirring up for them, she wished she had the courage to tell the truth before it went too far. But she was concerned about Tobias's health, and fancied that Alex's lie was trivial in itself, compared with the strife she might cause by bringing it into the open.

* * *

Going down to the library later, Cassie was nervous to the point of trepidation, and paused abruptly when she entered the book-lined room because Adam was seated at the desk by the window.

'I'm sorry,' she said quickly. 'Have I disturbed you? I am looking for Alex.'

Adam looked up. He was so much like Alex that it was difficult for her to accept that this was indeed a brother and not Alex himself playing a joke.

Adam smiled and, getting up, came towards her.

'You're not disturbing me at all,' he assured her. 'In fact I'm glad you've dropped in because we need to have a chat before your holiday begins in earnest.'

'Really?' She looked up into his face, keenly aware of his nearness, and the expression in his eyes brought a flush to her cheeks.

'You seem to be on the defensive,' he remarked. 'What has Alex been telling you about me?'

'Certainly nothing derogatory. Do you think he would slander you?' She smiled. 'Or would he have been telling the truth if he spoke of bad habits?'

His gaze narrowed and he made a small gesture of impatience. 'Knowing Alex, I would expect him to go around with a girl who matched him temperamentally, who likes the pleasure spots and the time wasting in which he indulges. He doesn't take kindly to the idea of working for a living and, up until now, Grandfather and I have tolerated his attitude and turned a blind eye to his playboy ways.'

'That has nothing to do with me!' She spoke firmly. 'I can see that you have cause for complaint about the way Alex leaves you here, but surely you should talk to him about that rather than a stranger!'

'You're hardly a stranger. If you and Alex intend marriage then you are already a part of the family, and must expect to be treated as such.' He shrugged. 'I can't get through to Alex, and if he loves you then I can only hope that you have some influence over him. If you are a responsible person you will do what you can to help me sway that brother of mine.'

She watched him intently, fascinated against her will. He was so like Alex but his mannerisms were far removed from Alex's. This man was more serious and obviously dedicated to the Mayfield way of life.

Cassie dearly wanted to explain to him that Alex had compromised her with Tobias, and that now she could only go along with what had been said, but she remained silent, aware that Alex must have been desperate to stage the lie they were now living.

'I think part of Alex's trouble is that you've all been too hard on him,' she mused. 'Perhaps he would settle down if you gave him half a chance. Have you ever considered that he lives the way he does because it's what you and his grandfather expect of him?'

'He's been given ample opportunity to come to his senses,' Adam informed her drily. 'Now time is getting short and Alex doesn't seem to realise that.

Grandfather is really beginning to feel his years. I don't think he'll live much longer unless he retires and takes things easy. If Alex settled down, Grandfather would certainly have a lot of worry lifted from his mind.'

'Perhaps Alex is planning to settle down now.' Cassie clenched her hands, aware that she was being pushed deeper into the deceitful situation Alex had created.

'You mean his forthcoming marriage to you?' Adam smiled and slowly shook his head. 'I'll believe that when it happens.'

She flushed, unable to find a retort.

'I know my brother far better than you ever will,' he continued, 'and I don't think he is the marrying kind. Frankly, I'm surprised he's shown up here with the story that you and he are considering matrimony.'

'So what do you think my motives are for coming with him?' Cassie asked, looking at him directly.

'That's your affair,' he answered. 'But

bear in mind that I am in the background watching, and I'll step in very quickly if it looks as if Grandfather might be upset by anything Alex does. Apart from that, enjoy your time here. Have your holiday, and leave it at that.' His gaze was suddenly unfriendly, and when she turned to leave he reached out and held her wrist. 'I hoped I could get you on my side,' he went on. 'Alex might just listen to you. So make him understand how poorly Grandfather is. The old man would like Alex to remain at home now he has returned, and if you have any decency at all you'll try to keep Alex here.'

Cassie regarded him unhappily. 'You say you know Alex better than me so you must be aware that no one in the world can make him do anything he hasn't a mind to.'

'If he's in love with you then he will listen.' Adam's eyes were shrewd, and his grasp upon her wrist caused Cassie to catch her breath, not because he was holding her too tightly, but because his touch seemed to do something to her. Their closeness had started her pulses racing. She tried to break away but he held her motionless, with no effort.

'I am concerned about Alex and his attitude towards life,' she said tensely. 'Naturally, I want to see him succeed, but he has never given himself the chance, mainly because no one around here will take him seriously. If you met him halfway you might be surprised by his reaction. Instead of trying to influence him, why don't you offer him more responsibility? I can assure you that the business he handled in England was very well done.'

'Mention extra responsibility to Alex and he'd disappear on the next flight to Europe!' Adam retorted. 'In this world no one should expect to get something for nothing, but Alex does.'

'I agree with you.' Cassie felt curiously breathless. She had stopped trying to break his grip and could only stand and gaze at him. 'But I won't try to influence him,' she continued firmly.

'That would be wrong. I see your problem as a family matter, and I'm not a Mayfield yet. In fact, you seem to think that I'll never become a member of your family. Anyway, whatever Alex does is his affair and has nothing to do with me.'

'So that's the basis for your marriage, is it? Well, Alex is responsible for this state of affairs so he has only himself to blame if things go wrong and the roof falls in on him.' He stared at her for a few moments longer before speaking again. 'I don't think you are really in love with Alex, so what are you after?'

'What do you know of love?' She was troubled by her reactions to his nearness, but now his rudeness brought on anger.

'What does anyone know of love?' He pulled her close. His brown eyes were narrowed, and she felt his breath against her cheek.

'Let me go!' she cried. 'You are Alex's brother. How dare you act like this! What kind of man are you?'

He slid his arms around her shoulders. 'I am my own kind of man,' he said softly. 'And I am not likely to forget that Alex is my brother. There are strong ties between us.'

'I don't know what you expect me to do!' She drew a deep breath.

Adam's features might have been chiselled out of granite. He gazed into her eyes, weakening her resolve so that she felt strangely indecisive. The heat in the room became oppressive.

She closed her eyes, and would have fallen if he had not caught her around the waist. She slumped against him. She couldn't hold up her head and her legs were growing curiously leaden and lifeless. Her face rested against his shoulder as she struggled to maintain her equilibrium, and he looked at her swiftly, sensing that something was wrong.

He swept her into his arms as if she were a child and carried her to a sofa. When he placed her upon it she opened her eyes and tried to focus upon his face. There was concern in his expression as she fought against the dizzy feeling which assailed her.

'What's going on?' Alex's cool voice spoke from the doorway.

'Cassie's having a bit of a faint.' Adam threw a glance over his shoulder at his brother before returning his attention to Cassie. 'Come and hold her hand while I get a glass of water. It's the change of climate, I expect.'

Cassie tried to ease herself into a sitting position. Heat enveloped her.

Adam moved away and Alex appeared in his place, frowning.

'It's all right, really,' she told him. 'All I need is some air!'

'Right, let's get you outside.' Alex picked her up and carried her to the french windows.

Adam had anticipated the move and was there to open them. He remained inside the library when Alex carried Cassie out to the terrace, and she began to breathe more easily in the less oppressive air as Alex lowered her feet to the ground then supported her.

'I'm sorry, Alex.' Cassie began to recover her poise. 'I was talking to Adam and all of a sudden I felt quite light-headed.'

'He does have that effect on some women!' Alex grinned, then sobered. 'You're not accustomed to the climate, that's all. But you'll be all right. Just don't try to do too much too soon.' He paused and threw a glance over his shoulder before continuing. 'Adam wasn't brow-beating you, was he?'

'How do you mean?' She lifted a hand to her clammy forehead.

'I know how Adam acts.' His tone was sharp. 'I thought perhaps he had started giving you a bad time.'

'You have a guilty conscience,' she reproved, 'and so you should have. This is an intolerable situation, Alex. And you're the one who's giving me a hard time. You've told lies about our relationship, and placed me in an unenviable position. I don't think I can go along with it.'

'I can't go back on the story now,' he told her, earnestly. 'And it will only be for the month you're holidaying here. Later we can say that we've decided against marriage and are splitting up when we get back to London. That way, no one will get hurt.'

She studied him, her expression serious. 'You know, Alex,' she said, 'I've gone along with you right from the start because I like you. But you only brought me here because I might be useful to you. I also have the feeling that when this holiday is over you'll take me back to England and forget I ever existed.'

'Don't worry about the future,' he told her cheerfully. 'You're only here for a month and you should make the most of it. We are friends, good friends, and nothing will ever change that.'

She frowned, experiencing a sinking feeling inside. He seemed to be under considerable stress but she couldn't tell if he was putting on an act for her benefit. They were friends, she agreed, and as such she couldn't help worrying about him.

'Look, why don't you go and have a rest?' Alex's attention was already moving on. 'Grandfather won't be up yet. You have until about seven-thirty before anyone will expect to see you again.' He glanced at his watch. 'That gives you plenty of time in which to recover.'

'I don't want to rest,' she protested. 'All I need is fresh air.'

'Well, I have things to do, Cassie,' he said, smiling. 'You may be on holiday but I'm not. I think you'll be all right until I get back. Just take it easy here in the garden, if you must have fresh air. I'll tell Martha to keep an eye on you. If Adam does come to talk, just try to be extra nice to him. I'm going to need all the support I can get.'

Cassie gazed after his tall figure as he left her but it was Adam who loomed in her mind, and she shivered despite the heat because of the effect he had upon her. It was apparent that he could affect her as no other man had done before, and that made him extremely dangerous.

She walked amidst the colourful flower-beds, her thoughts busy, her emotions in chaos, for no matter which way she turned there was one inescapable thought in her mind. Already she was aching to see Adam again and experience the thrill of his company, and yet she was uneasy because her emotions could betray her . . .

3

It was just before seven-thirty that evening when Alex tapped at Cassie's door. She turned from her position at the window where she had been looking at the exotic scenery, and Alex emitted a low whistle, for she was wearing a lemon, off-the-shoulder dress that showed her shapely figure to perfection. Her blonde hair was groomed in an intricate style that enhanced the shape of her face.

'You look great, Cassie!' he exclaimed. 'Are you ready for the slaughter? Grandfather and Adam are downstairs, and Simone has been invited as company for you.'

'Oh!' Cassie thought of the woman who had entered the bedroom that afternoon and immediately feared that she would be at an even greater disadvantage in her company. So now, she thought resignedly, instead of just Adam watching her for the slightest mistake, Simone would be there as well, claws unsheathed.

'You're not nervous, are you?' Alex asked. He looked searchingly into her blue eyes. 'There's nothing to worry about, you know. Just take your lead from me.'

'That's all very well,' she protested, 'but I never know what you're going to say next! All I do know is that you'll hurt your grandfather very badly if you're not careful, and I really resent being dragged into this situation and made to play a part.'

'All you'll have to do this evening is sit at the table and look beautiful.' He smiled disarmingly. 'You'll charm Adam, then I'll talk about my plans. It's only this evening that you'll need to be on your guard. After that, you can relax and enjoy your holiday.'

She was far from convinced, and there was a sinking sensation in her breast as they went down to the lounge, where Adam and Simone were chatting to Tobias. Both men rose to their feet as Alex ushered Cassie into the room.

'What would you like to drink, Cassie?' Adam moved to a large cabinet, his dark eyes already compelling her gaze. 'We have a few moments before dinner.'

'I know what she likes,' Alex cut in. 'I'll get it.' He crossed to Adam's side, and Cassie was confused as she tried to reconcile the man she knew with the comparative stranger who was making such demands upon her emotions.

'Are you feeling better now, Cassie?' Tobias asked, coming to her side.

He led her to a low settee, and she was startled to find his fingers cold on her arm. They sat together, and Cassie was relieved, as she looked into his dark eyes, that Adam couldn't seat himself beside her.

Tobias was smiling, and his fatherly air immediately eased her tension.

'I'm feeling more settled now, thank you,' she replied to his question. 'And how are you? Does this heat bother you at all?'

'Yes, it does, and more these days than it used to,' he replied. 'Truth to tell, for some months now I've been toying with the idea of going back to England to spend the rest of my days. If I had any sense I'd retire and start getting some fun out of life before it's too late.'

'You've never mentioned retirement to me.' Adam came forward. 'It would kill you, Tobias, to have to leave this place,' he added.

'I could leave with an easy conscience if Alex settled down to the business and pulled his weight,' Tobias answered.

Cassie glanced at Alex and saw that he was making a big thing of talking to Simone.

'If Alex does settle down then it won't be before time,' Adam observed. He glanced at his brother but Alex had no intention of being drawn on that subject. Equally, Adam would not let him wriggle out of anything. 'Alex,' he said, 'don't keep us in suspense. What are your plans exactly? And I'm not talking about marriage.' He glanced at Cassie and smiled.

'This is neither the time nor the place to talk business,' Alex responded, and Cassie saw him moisten his lips nervously. She tensed as he continued. 'I do have one or two irons in the fire back in Europe, but we can talk that over tomorrow.'

'That should be most interesting.' Adam smiled, but Cassie noticed his expression had sharpened. 'Are we to take it then that you're not planning to settle out here?'

'Nothing is settled yet!' Alex spoke defensively, for he hadn't counted on being cornered so soon.

Martha saved him. She appeared in the doorway to announce that dinner was ready.

Tobias immediately arose, offered Cassie his arm and led her to the dining-room. Adam followed them closely, leaving Alex to escort Simone.

Then began what proved to be an ordeal for Cassie. During the meal, Adam kept chipping at Alex, returning time and again to the subject of future plans despite Alex's efforts to avoid it. When Adam became too insistent for Alex's nerve a tension became apparent, and Tobias, seemingly reluctantly, tabooed the whole subject of business.

Cassie, watching points closely, realised that Tobias was obviously unwell, and accepted that she would have to carry on with the lie she was living, if only to spare the older man any kind of shock.

Adam was making her feel uneasy again by watching her intently. Whenever her gaze strayed in his direction he seemed to be studying her.

Alex managed to stay out of trouble by talking almost nonstop about his travels in Europe, and Cassie was appalled by the way he exaggerated the success of the business he had handled. She felt embarrassed for him, aware that Adam wasn't being fooled in the slightest.

Then Simone, who had been listening intently to the by-play between the brothers, asked Cassie some pointed questions about her love affair with Alex, and, in no time at all, Cassie was floundering.

'Have you lost your ring?' Simone asked unexpectedly.

'Ring?' Cassie was momentarily nonplussed.

'Your engagement ring. If you and Alex are planning marriage then surely you have become engaged.' Simone's dark eyes glinted as she glanced at Cassie's bare left hand before looking meaningly at Adam.

Cassie threw an appealing glance toward Alex, but almost immediately transferred her gaze to Adam's firmly set features, feeling certain again that he knew the truth of the situation, and that fear unnerved her far more than any other consideration. She was relieved when Alex eventually came to her rescue.

'I promised Cassie a ring from the shop where Father bought Mother's ring,' he said with great aplomb.

'That's uncharacteristically sentimental of you.' Adam was toying with a long-stemmed wine glass, his brown eyes filled with speculation. 'You did say you haven't set a date for your wedding, didn't you?'

'For heaven's sake!' Alex refused to be bullied. 'We haven't set a firm date, if you're really interested. Cassie has to decide if she would like to live in this part of the world before we can get down to any serious planning. I seem to be doing nothing but keep trying to explain why we're here,' Alex added huffily. 'No decisions have been made yet. It's not the first time I've told you, Adam, so why don't you lay off? It's really none of your business. You'll be informed of our plans the moment we do decide something.'

Cassie began to fear that Alex would lose his temper, which seemed to be the reaction Adam was aiming for. She noted that Tobias sat motionless at the head of the table, apparently disinterested in the conversation, but his keen eyes were watchful, and she realised that it would be a mistake to underestimate or discount him.

She fancied that Tobias and Adam had arranged this cross-examination. She could understand Adam wanting Alex to shoulder his share of the burden of running the family business, and if Alex's agreement to do so was necessary for Tobias's future plans then there was just reason for them all to be concerned.

'Tell us about the interests you have in the European markets,' Adam suggested, unmoved by Alex's outburst, and Cassie saw Alex squirm in his seat.

'I've got some facts and figures up in my room,' he replied slowly. 'I'll get them out tomorrow and we can go over them.'

'Do we know any of the people involved?' Adam persisted.

'Among other people, Leon Hilliard has afforded me the opportunity of buying into Consolidated Textiles.' Alex leaned back in his seat and, when he glanced at Cassie, his face was almost as red as the wine he was drinking.

'Leon Hilliard!' Tobias exploded, shocking Cassie with his vehemence. 'I wouldn't do business with him if he were the last man on earth!'

'I see!' Alex slammed his glass on the table so hard that it toppled over and sent a long red tongue of wine across the spotless cloth. He sprang to his feet, almost overturning his chair in the process. 'Nothing ever changes, does it?' he demanded. 'Even when I do try to get into business someone has to belittle my efforts! Is it any wonder that I'm reluctant to come back here and settle down?'

He glared at Tobias, then looked at Adam as if to challenge him to make some remark. When there was no reaction from either man he turned and strode from the room, despite Adam's

67

sharp command to remain.

Cassie sat motionless, hands clasped in her lap, certain that Alex was playing some kind of a deep game with his family because he had mentioned more than once back in England that he wouldn't touch any business of Leon Hilliard's with a barge pole! But perhaps he didn't want to be questioned too closely at the moment about his true business activities and this was his way of avoiding it!

Cassie suppressed a sigh for the silence that ensured was heavy, overwhelming, and she was aware that Adam's gaze still remained upon her.

'If you will excuse me,' Tobias said wearily, 'I'll go up to my room. I think it was a mistake for me to put in an appearance this evening.' He looked apologetically in Cassie's direction. 'Please forgive our bad manners, Cassie,' he pleaded. 'It's a cardinal sin to discuss business matters at the table, but Adam and I have been so impatiently awaiting Alex's return. No doubt you are aware of how dilatory he is in business matters. But I'll talk to him tomorrow, when he'll be less tired from travelling.

'I do hope you'll enjoy your holiday on the island. Any time Alex is busy, perhaps Adam will keep you company.'

'Thank you.' Cassie glanced at Adam, and was surprised to see that he was smiling. He seemed pleased with the way Alex had been discomfited, and she tried to figure out whether or not he was malicious.

Tobias left the room, and Simone rose to her feet when Adam nodded his head slightly, an action which Cassie saw and understood.

Simone walked casually to the door although her expression showed great reluctance. 'I have to be running along,' she said. 'I'll probably see you tomorrow, Adam.' Her tone hardened slightly as she glanced at him, but she smiled over-sweetly at Cassie. 'I hope you'll enjoy your stay on Tarango, Cassie. Make Alex show you the sights. Don't let him shirk his duty.'

'Thank you.' Cassie arose from the table as Simone departed.

'Don't go yet,' Adam spoke curtly. 'I want to talk to you.'

'I don't think we have anything to discuss,' she said coldly, 'and I'd rather get some air.' She continued around the table, having to pass his chair, and he stood up before she reached him, then grasped her wrist.

'Let me go!' she said firmly. 'I have nothing to say to you. I think you were most unfair to Alex this evening, and nothing you can say will make me want to help change his mind about anything.'

'So you're already under Alex's thumb!' Adam's eyes glinted. 'One word from him and you unsheath your claws in his defence. I am surprised. You don't look as if you'd be the dutiful little wife who believes her husband is always right.'

'It may be that what is right for Alex is not right for you,' she retorted. 'You could at least go thoroughly into his business plans before condemning or ridiculing his choice of partners,' she added scathingly.

'We have experienced some of Alex's wheeling and dealing before.' There was cold amusement in his eyes. 'If we left him to his own devices he'd very soon bankrupt us with his perverted business acumen.'

'Now,' he continued, 'as to talking to you, it has nothing to do with Alex. I'd like to know something about you personally, coming, as you are, into the Mayfield family.'

'I should think you already know about me,' she responded. 'Seeing the suspicious mind you have, I can believe that you've had a dossier on me compiled and sent out from England.'

He smiled and shook his head in disbelief, and she couldn't help but notice how strikingly handsome he was. It was rather more than mere physical appeal, she realised. Adam possessed a masculinity that was irresistible.

She wanted to be angry with him, for, as she saw it, Alex hadn't been given a fair hearing, despite his track record in business. She felt that if he were encouraged more, given responsibility and trusted implicitly, he might settle comfortably to working in the family business. She looked into Adam's face and saw that he was studying her, eyes glinting with what looked suspiciously like amusement.

'So you're the daughter of William Overton,' he said quietly. 'He was on the island a couple of years ago. He and my grandfather have known each other for years, and I believe they were business associates at one time.' He nodded slowly. 'I'll assume that you didn't make friends with Alex because of his position and money, being of the Overton family. So perhaps you are in love with him, after all.'

'Thank you very much!' Cassie wrenched herself out of his grasp and stepped back. Anger filled her and she was tempted to slap his face, but he came forward again, this time placing both hands around her waist.

'I have a responsibility to my family,' he said. 'If Alex got caught up with the wrong type of woman it could cost us a fortune. Thank goodness he hasn't been that foolish in his travels.'

'I think I'd better go and look for Alex,' Cassie said, keenly aware of his thumbs pressing her waist as she tried to twist away. 'And I think you should keep your distance, don't you? What are you trying to do, test my fidelity? I am engaged to your brother, remember.'

'I'm not likely to forget that.' He smiled. 'Do you really love Alex?'

'That's a strange question, considering that I'm engaged to be married to him.'

'You don't look or act as if you're in love with him. If you were my fiancée, I'd expect much more from you.'

'I don't doubt that! You're the kind of man who would take what he wanted and give nothing in return. I don't think I like your attitude, Adam.'

'You don't have to like me at all! It's Alex you're planning to marry!' He smiled, released her suddenly and walked away.

She went thoughtfully in search of Alex, aware that his little subterfuge was childish in the face of broader issues, and the sooner he put their relationship into its true perspective the better for all concerned. But there was no sign of him in the house, and, when she became tired of looking, she decided to call it a day.

* * *

When she awoke the next morning, Cassie found the sun coming in at the window almost intolerably brilliant, and had to open her eyes by degrees. She then glanced at her wristwatch and a gasp of shock escaped her. The time was almost ten! She must have slept the clock round! Springing out of bed, she dashed into the bathroom.

After showering, she donned shorts

and a loose top, pushed her feet into sandals and brushed her blonde hair. She left her bedroom and went in search of Alex. When she failed to locate him, she wandered into the kitchen.

'Miss Cassie! Come in and sit at the table.' Martha appeared in the doorway leading from the back porch. 'Masta Alex wanted to call you early but I warned him to let you lie and take your time. You're gonna need several days to get used to our climate, and if you try to rush it, you could make yourself ill. Now tell me, is there anything you would like for breakfast?'

'A cereal please, Martha,' Cassie responded.

'Well, sit right down and I'll attend to you. How do you like your coffee?'

'Black, with no sugar, please.' Cassie looked around the large, modern kitchen as she sat down at a corner of the long table. 'Have you any idea where Alex is?' she asked. 'He doesn't seem to be around.'

'He left a message for you. He has a busy day ahead, so you'd better make your own amusement.' Martha shrugged expressively. 'That's the trouble with the Mayfields. Business is the be all and end all with them, and women have to take second place. What was you hopin' to do this mornin', honey?'

'Nothing special.' Cassie smiled. 'I'd really like to go down to the beach. We were at the beginning of winter when I left England, so all of this is like an enchanting dream.'

'I've sent Eltina, the maid, down to the beach house in the cove because I figured you'd like to go down there this mornin'. She'll be keepin' an eye on things while you're there. So enjoy yourself. You're on holiday, and you mustn't let Masta Alex's business activities throw you off.'

'I won't.' Cassie began to eat her cereal, and fought against asking after Adam.

She could feel the urge to see him

despite her attempts to smother it. If she had any sense, she told herself sternly, she would do her utmost to avoid him. But why should she? The question sprang readily to her mind. She was not engaged to marry Alex! But equally she couldn't permit her natural feelings to evolve normally because everyone thought that she and Alex were in love!

'Can you drive, Miss Cassie?' Martha inquired. 'It's six miles to the beach and you'll have to use one of the buggies.'

'Yes, I can drive.' Cassie nodded.

'That's fine. When you've eaten your breakfast, I'll show you where the buggy is and give you directions for reachin' the cove. Did you bring your swimwear? There will be towels at the beach house.'

'I've a bikini in my room. I'll fetch it when I've finished my breakfast.'

Martha nodded then left her, and, after breakfast, Cassie went to get her bikini. She met Tobias on the stairs.

'Good morning, Tobias,' she greeted

him. 'How are you feeling today?'

'Good morning, Cassie.' His face was deep-lined, and the fact that he was not in the best of health showed clearly. 'I didn't sleep too well. The heat keeps me awake, you know. I envy the weather they have in London at the moment.'

Cassie smiled. 'When I left London it was raining, and there was a forecast of sleet and snow showers,' she told him. 'That kind of weather wouldn't do you much good.'

He smiled in return then changed the subject. 'I hope we're going to be friends, Cassie. I'm sorry if the atmosphere at dinner last evening gave you the wrong impression of us. We are experiencing a family crisis at the moment, and I'm hoping that Alex will help us through it.'

'I'm sorry to hear that. I sensed the tension last night, and I can't help wondering if you're not judging Alex too harshly. I have known him for some time now, and had the opportunity to see the way he handled business in

England. To tell you the truth I couldn't fault him anywhere, so perhaps your doubts are unfounded.'

'Well said!' He nodded at her in approval. 'My trouble is that I've become too old to bother with the details as I did in the past. Alex is all right and I'm sorry I spoke the way I did about his contacts. Where is he, do you know? I'd like to have a serious chat with him.'

'I'm afraid I don't know where he is. He left a message for me to make my own amusement today, so I'm going down to the beach.'

'But you're on holiday,' he protested. 'Alex shouldn't go off and leave you to your own devices.'

'Please, it doesn't matter. I antici-pated spending some time on my own while I'm here. Alex isn't on holiday. Perhaps he didn't make that clear yesterday. He has work to do. I'll be quite all right alone.' She could tell by his expression that he didn't wholly agree. She was momentarily tempted to blurt out the truth, but it was obvious that to do so would only make the situation seem much worse than it really was.

'I suppose you're right.' He spoke doubtfully. 'I just don't understand young people these days. I'm sure I never treated my fiancée like that when I was Alex's age.' He moved to go down the stairs then paused. 'What you ought to do is get Adam to show you around. You shouldn't have to explore alone.'

'It's all right,' she insisted. 'I enjoy solitude.' She continued on her way, collected the bikini, then returned to the kitchen.

Martha showed her to a buggy and gave her explicit directions for getting to the cove.

Cassie waved a hand as she drove off, and after a few moments she became familiar with the controls and steered around the house to the beach path. Driving steadily, she found it pleasant motoring under the trees that covered the long slope down to the coast.

Several times she sped out into the open, passed across some fields, and then slid under the trees again. The open top of the vehicle permitted the slipstream to cool her face, and she was exhilarated by the time she reached the cove.

The path continued across firm white sand, tyre tracks plainly indicating in which direction she should drive. There were palm trees growing out of the beach, and she slowed in order to look around. The path then veered to the right and she saw the sea, sparkling blue and calm as a pond.

To the right there was a wooden beach house with a veranda, and a tall slender native girl was sitting in a rocking chair in the shade.

The girl arose when the vehicle appeared, and smiled as Cassie stopped the buggy and sprang out.

'Hello. You're Eltina, aren't you?' Cassie asked.

'Yes, Miss. If there's anything you want then just ask.'

'All I need is a place to change then into the sea,' Cassie responded.

Eltina showed her into the beach house and Cassie changed into her black bikini. The native girl provided a large beach towel, then Cassie drove the three hundred yards to the water's edge. Glancing around, it amazed her that she didn't see another living soul anywhere. When she tested the water she couldn't believe it could be so warm. With great pleasure she dived in and began swimming in the crystal clear depths.

This was more like it, she thought as she floated on her back. She was compelled to keep her eyes closed because the sun was so brilliant. In the background the sound of large waves crashing upon a reef across the mouth of the cove lulled her with its insistence. She swam again, finding that she could open her eyes under the surface and see many wonders of the marine world. After a while, she left the water and spread the towel on the hard white sand.

Within minutes she realised that she couldn't take too much sun at the outset, and arose with great reluctance to drive back to the beach house and change.

Eltina gave her a cold drink, and later they both chatted animatedly on the drive back to the house.

When they reached the terrace, Cassie looked around for Alex, but Martha appeared, and in reply to Cassie's question, informed her that he hadn't yet returned.

'Take my advice and rest,' the housekeeper suggested. 'You're looking a bit peaked, Miss Cassie, so don't overdo it.'

'Thanks, I'm sure you're right, Martha,' Cassie agreed. 'I'll take a shower and change, then have something to eat, perhaps. I'll come down to the kitchen shortly.'

She was eating a light meal in the kitchen when Adam entered. He was wearing riding-breeches, boots, and an open-neck brown shirt. She watched him flip a wide-brimmed hat on to a nearby chair as he sat down opposite.

Martha hastened to pour him a cold beer.

'Alex left you in the lurch this morning, did he?' he demanded.

'He certainly didn't,' Cassie replied indignantly. 'What gave you that idea?'

He chuckled and ignored her question. 'Are you doing anything special this afternoon?' he asked. 'I have to ride over to the Marchant estate and wouldn't mind some company. Can you ride?'

'Yes, although I haven't done so for a long time.' Cassie spoke doubtfully.

'Have you any riding clothes?'

'Oh yes. Alex insisted that I bring some.'

'Then go and change while I select a horse for you.' He studied her for a moment. 'I'll be leaving in thirty minutes. Can you be ready by then?'

'Certainly.' She stifled a retort which rose to her lips and muttered, 'Thanks,' then left the kitchen before he could comment further and went up to her room to change into riding clothes, all thoughts of rest forgotten.

★　★　★

When she was riding across the fields with Adam, Cassie began to feel the full effects of the heat, even though he kept to the shade of the trees where possible. She soon began to see another side to him, too. He talked business, and she quickly learned the scope and extent of Mayfield interests. She realised that he was a very hard-working man, and it was no wonder that he resented the way Alex travelled around the world in search of pleasure while he was anchored to the island by business responsibilities.

She was interested in what he was telling her and because he wasn't criticising Alex or sniping at her, she could enjoy his company.

'We're crossing the boundary between

our place and the Marchant estate,' he said at length. 'I'm hoping to set up a company with Simone's father, Pierre, and run a holiday complex on an island not far from here. I think it could become a great success and the profits would be high.'

'You make it sound as if it's all right for your business ideas and projects, but Alex gets the thumbs down on principle if he has the temerity to suggest anything,' Cassie remarked.

Adam glanced at her, surprised, then frowned. He slowed his horse until it was merely walking, and she did likewise.

'I appreciate your loyalty to the man you are planning to marry,' Adam observed then, 'but please don't lump my business ideas together with the kind of hare-brained schemes that Alex intermittently breeds. What do you know about business, anyway? Oh, but of course! You're a whizz-kid Sales Director! I do apologise!' He broke off and raised a hand to shield his eyes.

'That looks like Simone up there,' he commented. 'I need to talk to her. Keep riding along this path while I chase after her. I'll catch up with you again before you can reach the Marchant house.'

Before she could agree or protest, he spurred the horse and galloped away. Cassie raised her eyes to see a distant rider on the point of disappearing over the brow of a hill. Continuing at a steady pace, she told herself that his arrogance was too much! He acted as if he had the only business brain in the world. No wonder Alex found him frustrating.

She followed the path he had indicated, still thinking about him, and tried to persuade herself that she didn't really like him, but there was a tiny part of an indefinable emotion in her mind, which niggled and demanded attention. It made her restive and she twisted in her saddle and looked around for him but the fields were empty, completely devoid of life. She stood up in her stirrups to peer ahead for a glimpse of the Marchant house.

Hoofbeats startled her and she twisted in the saddle, looking eagerly for Adam. Her eyes narrowed when she saw Simone approaching. The girl was riding furiously, exhibiting a great deal of skill, and the spirited bay upon which she was mounted would need a lot of control, Cassie realised. The animal almost lost its footing as it reached level ground, and Simone picked it up magnificently.

Cassie reined in, for Simone was coming towards her, and she held the reins tightly when her quiet mare moved nervously at the top of a precipitous slope that dropped into a steep ravine.

'What are you doing here?' Simone demanded, pulling her horse to a halt beside Cassie.

'I'm with Adam. He spotted you back there a few moments ago and rode to intercept you. We're on our way to visit your father.'

'I see.' Simone was patently displeased. 'What are you doing with Adam? Why aren't you out with Alex?'

Cassie decided not to answer that. It was bad enough having to suffer Adam's arrogance but Simone wasn't even connected with Alex's family, although she had set herself up in an antagonistic role.

'I'll continue riding,' Cassie said. 'Perhaps you want to go back and meet Adam. He went off to the left.'

'He knows his way around,' Simone retorted. 'I'm going home, and I'm in a hurry!'

Cassie shrugged and turned away to ride on, but her horse seemed to lose its footing on the rough ground. It snorted then reared violently, taking Cassie completely by surprise. She gasped in horror as she vacated the saddle in a flailing arc, flinging her arms wide, her fingers clawing at empty space. The ground came up to meet her and she tried to relax, to soften the impact, but made contact with a terrific jolt.

There was a sharp pain in her forehead, then blackness swirled inside to engulf her and she lost consciousness . . .

4

When Cassie came to her senses, she was lying in the shade of a tree with Adam kneeling beside her. Opening her eyes, she closed them again quickly because the glare of the sun was overwhelming. She groaned, painfully aware of a sharp pain in her head, and when she tried to move she suffered a bout of dizziness.

'Don't move, Cassie!' Adam commanded, alerted by her movement.

She opened her eyes the merest slits and looked up at him, experiencing a desire to sit up. She struggled against his restraining hand for he misunderstood her action and tried to keep her motionless.

'I must sit up,' she protested weakly.

'I've checked you over and nothing seems to be broken,' he said, as if her body was a car or some other piece of machinery. Then his hands slid under her shoulders and she was lifted into a sitting position. Her head rested against his shoulder. 'That was a stupid thing to do,' he commented. 'You shouldn't have gone within ten feet of that slope.'

Cassie opened her eyes and looked around. There was no sign of Simone.

'Help me to my feet, please,' she begged. 'I feel a little dizzy.'

'No way,' he retorted. 'You're concussed. Just stay still. I've sent Simone for a car, and we'll take you to the hospital for a check-up.' He paused and frowned at her. 'What on earth were you trying to do, kill yourself?'

'Kill myself?' She was startled. 'I didn't do anything!'

'Simone told me what happened. She saw it all. You turned your horse at the top of the slope and it reared because it was frightened.'

Cassie overcame the dizziness and opened her eyes fully to look at his tanned face. She pushed herself from him and tried to scramble to her feet.

Adam rose as she straightened, and had to catch her when she swayed and closed her eyes. The next instant she was pressed against his chest and his strong hands held her motionless.

'Don't you ever do as you're told?' he demanded. 'How do you think I would have felt if you'd been seriously hurt? You were in my care. I'm supposed to be looking after you.'

'Don't get huffy with me!' she said coldly. 'It's not my fault you saw Simone and took out after her. If you are so concerned about me getting hurt then you shouldn't have left me, should you?' She was keenly aware of being held in his arms.

'I'm not going to hospital,' she added then. 'If you will just please help me back into the saddle, I'll ride home.' She looked at him defiantly as she spoke.

'You're not going to ride back,' he insisted. 'Don't be an idiot, Cassie. You're concussed, and should go straight to hospital. Whatever you may think of me, I do have your welfare at heart.'

Cassie was preparing to argue when a Land Rover appeared on the track and pulled up beside them. Her senses receded then and she was only dimly aware that Adam swung her into his arms and lifted her bodily into the vehicle.

She endured the lurching, jolting trip back to the house with her eyes closed and her face pressed against Adam's shoulder. But slowly her discomfort eased and she began to recollect her thoughts.

She heard Simone's voice from time to time, also a man's, a stranger who spoke with a French accent. Simone's father, she assumed but she was too bemused to care about what was going on around her.

When the vehicle finally stopped, Adam began to lift her out. She heard Alex's voice in the background and immediately felt relieved.

Opening her eyes, she saw Alex's face

expressing concern. He took her from Adam and carried her into the house. She closed her eyes and remained quiet until Alex lowered her gently to a settee in the drawing-room.

Martha's voice was sounding in the background, angry and accusing. Someone suggested sending for the doctor, and Cassie sighed and gave up the unequal struggle to retain her senses. A black hole seemed to open up in her mind and she was lost in a blissful void . . .

★ ★ ★

The next time she opened her eyes it was to find herself in bed, with a stranger sitting on a chair at her side. He was middle-aged, dressed in a brown suit, and had a kindly face and shrewd blue eyes. He smiled reassuringly when he saw that she had regained consciousness.

'Hello,' he said pleasantly, getting to his feet and bending over her. 'I'm Doctor Stephenson. You have nothing to worry about, Cassie. Fortunately there are no bones broken but you are concussed, and I want you to remain in bed until tomorrow at least. Now I'd like to examine your eyes.'

He was silent while examining her, and she winced when his firm fingers pressed insistently around the bump on her forehead. 'I don't think we have any problems there.' His tone exuded confidence. 'The bruise is turning out nicely. But falling off a horse is not the best way to get to know the country, is it?'

'I agree.' Cassie smiled wanly. 'Thank you, Doctor. I'm sure I shall be all right now.'

'Just take it easy for a few days,' he advised. 'I'll leave some tablets for you to take — two every four hours. I suspect that you have a headache at the moment, but it should be gone by morning. However, if it persists longer than two days then let me know and I'll visit you again.'

He departed, and Cassie closed her

eyes. Her head was still aching dully and she felt shocked.

She was still reliving the incident when the door opened and Alex spoke.

'Are you awake, Cassie?'

'Yes. Come in.' She opened her eyes and gazed at him as he crossed to the side of the bed.

'Well! You're the clever one, aren't you?' he said. 'What on earth happened?'

She related the incident, and he sighed and shook his head.

'Adam shouldn't have left you,' he said severely, then, surprisingly, he chuckled harshly. 'This will give me the opportunity to have a go at him, you know.'

'Well, don't worry about me!' she gasped. 'You go ahead and concentrate on your feud with Adam, and if anyone gets hurt on the sidelines then that's just too bad!'

He grimaced. 'Sorry,' he said contritely. 'It wasn't meant how it sounded. I am appalled by what happened. It was too bad of Adam, Cassie. But it's no more than one can expect from him. He's so careless around women, and very cautious about himself.

'There was a girl I brought home a few years ago. The moment she set eyes on Adam, she left me cold. And he had the devil of a job to get rid of her. In the end she threatened to kill herself if he didn't marry her.' He shook his head. 'That's why he's so defensive around women, but that's no excuse for letting you almost get killed.'

'Surely he doesn't think I'm suddenly going to throw myself at him!' Cassie exclaimed. Her senses swirled and she put a hand to her forehead. 'And he isn't in love with Simone, is he? When I saw them together last evening they didn't look as if they even liked each other, although I must admit that Simone warned me off him.'

Alex nodded. 'She'd certainly have something to say to you. She is rather possessive, and never gives up the hope that one day Adam will turn to her.'

'She's welcome to him!' Cassie fingered the bump on her forehead. 'He's too arrogant for me.'

He stared at her for a moment. 'So that's how you feel about him,' he observed. 'I must admit that he has an unfortunate manner but it's all a big act. He's not really like that inside.' He paused, then asked, 'Does he bore you?'

'That's the last thing he does.' She frowned as a picture of Adam's face appeared upon the screen of her mind. 'I really don't know what to make of him.' She was going to say more but changed her mind.

'Has he made a pass at you?'

'You sound as if that would please you.' Cassie looked at him with an exasperated expression. 'I don't understand you at all, Alex.'

'I'm sorry, Cassie,' he replied quickly, 'I'm not being fair to you. Listen, one of the reasons why I passed you off as my fiancée is because of Kirsty. I've told you about her, and one day I hope to marry her. The trouble is, her father and my grandfather are deadly business rivals and that's no exaggeration. Tobias won't have Kirsty within a mile of the place because he's certain she would spy for her father. It's utterly ridiculous, I know, but that's what the Mayfields are like when it comes to their business interests and fortune.

'The last time I was home, Grandfather became very suspicious about my romantic inclinations and that's why I brought you along and passed you off as my fiancée. While Tobias and Adam think I'm going to marry you, they won't suspect that I'm still seeing Kirsty. As a matter of fact, I was with Kirsty for most of today.'

'You're the limit, Alex.' Cassie shook her head, but she couldn't be angry with him. 'I don't mind helping you out, but you should have warned me about Adam.'

'He'll settle down in time. At the moment he's busy in his big brother role! But there's no malice in him. He's only concerned about Grandfather.'

'It's a pity you're not as concerned as Adam,' she responded. 'I'm worried about your grandfather, Alex. How is he going to take the truth when he finally learns of it?'

'Don't worry about that side of it. Just keep up the pretence for the moment and there'll be no problems. Trust me.' He patted her shoulder. 'Now why don't you get some rest? Martha is going to bring your tablets shortly.'

'Thanks,' Cassie sighed. 'What a fine holiday this is turning out to be.'

She slid down the bed and closed her eyes. He bent and kissed her lightly on the forehead before departing, and when he had gone she lay considering the situation yet again. Her head was still aching, and she tried to sleep.

Martha entered the room carrying a tray that contained a small bottle of tablets and a glass of water.

Cassie took two tablets then drifted into slumber despite the intensity of her thoughts. When she awoke later she was relieved to discover that she was apparently back to normal, apart from the bruise on her forehead. The headache was gone and her mind was clear.

She arose slowly and went in search of Alex, wanting to talk some more about his plans, aware that until she knew the full extent of them she couldn't decide for herself just how to play her part in this frustrating situation . . .

She discovered that Alex wasn't in the house, and went to look around the extensive gardens. As she stepped out to the terrace, Adam called to her.

'Cassie, just a moment!' He came quickly to her side when she paused and stared intently at her. 'You're looking much better now,' he commented. 'How do you feel?'

'Fine, thank you.' She'd made a vow to remain calm and self-possessed in his company, but wasn't finding it easy to do so. His dark eyes seemed to bore into her.

'Do you know where Alex is?' he asked.

She shook her head. 'I have no idea. I was just looking for him myself.'

'Then come with me. I feel like a walk and the air will do you good. Let's take that path over there.' He took her arm and escorted her across the terrace. 'I'd like to talk with you.'

As they stepped off the terrace and joined the path she wondered what was wrong with her. She had never felt so vulnerable before, and was actually enjoying the sensations Adam's presence aroused in her.

The air grew a little cooler as they walked along the path, and Cassie was relieved. Adam's hand upon her arm was a constant reminder of his presence, and she had to make an effort to resist the impulses that coursed through her.

'I'd like to talk about Alex,' he said shortly. 'I am extremely concerned about him. He's always been a problem but now matters are coming to a head and

103

I'm worried about Tobias, too.'

Cassie glanced at him, wondering at the change in him. Was he trying a different approach? She smiled inwardly at the thought, but chased emotion out of her expression when he met her gaze.

'I've never met a man like you before,' she commented.

He halted and placed his hands upon her shoulders. 'What exactly do you mean by that?'

She shook her head. 'I don't have to explain myself.'

There was no sunlight under the trees and the shade was strangely unrealistic. She looked into his dark eyes, and quickly realised that she was on dangerous ground.

'I think you should explain,' he said firmly.

'No, it doesn't matter. And we're supposed to be talking about Alex. You're not being fair to him, you know.' It needed an effort to change the subject but she did so. 'You say you

want him in your business but you
don't trust him. If you don't let him
have some responsibility then how can
he prove himself? What you do want, I
imagine, is the best of both worlds
— Alex here, where you can keep an
eye on him, yet not succeeding in
business.'

'So that's what you think of me!' His
gaze bored into her. 'Do you always
make snap judgments of the people you
meet? We didn't know each other
existed until recently so how can you
know what I'm like? I certainly don't
know anything about you yet, and I
pride myself upon the speed of my
perception.' He chuckled softly. 'So you
don't like me, and don't trust me!'

'I didn't say that! Anyway you
seemed to think you knew exactly what
kind of a woman I was at a glance. All
that talk about fearing for the Mayfield
fortune!' She spoke hotly, aware of
being on the defensive and knowing
that he was also aware of the fact.

The smile on his lips told her

everything. He thought he was controlling her, and if this was the way he dominated his twin brother then Alex had her sympathy and she could condone his falsehood about their relationship.

'First impressions.' He smiled. 'Well, my first impressions of you are confused. I don't think you are in love with Alex, so why are you engaged to him, if it isn't for money?'

'I do love Alex,' she countered, and frowned, for she was being stung into giving credence to Alex's lie. 'It's none of your business, but I do love him!'

'Yet you are disturbed by me. You feel uncomfortable in my company, so don't try to deny it.'

'You have a conceit that would be too big for an elephant,' she retorted. 'If I'm in any way uncomfortable it's only because you're so disconcerting!'

His hands slid around her body, drawing her into an embrace. She was crushed against his chest, and before she could protest his mouth found hers in the gloom and the world seemed to explode. Passion erupted inside her, and while a part of her mind tried to protest, the rest surrendered in a riot of pleasure and desire.

Then sanity returned and she twisted in an attempt to escape from him. He pressed a hand to the back of her head, imprisoning her against his mouth. She could hardly breathe, and intensified her resistance.

He released her unexpectedly and she twisted away, swaying, poised atop a pinnacle that was far too giddy for her habitually well-ordered mind.

She tried to think of something to say. She was shocked by the kiss, not so much because he was Alex's brother but by the way he had wrung a response from her.

'Well, at least you do have some human reactions in your make-up,' he said huskily, taking hold of her arm. He felt her momentary resistance and laughed lightly. 'Alex has my approval to marry you, if he wishes.'

'He certainly wishes to!' She was angered by his arrogance. 'And he doesn't need your consent or approval.' She paused before adding, 'I don't know what rules you live by out here, but where I come from a man doesn't kiss a future sister-in-law like that!'

'Oh dear! I've upset you!' He laughed, and she clenched her hands. 'I hope that doesn't mean we shall be enemies now. We should be on the same side, you know. For despite what you may think, I do have Alex's best interests at heart.'

'I'm aware that if you thought I wasn't suitable for him you'd do your best to get rid of me despite his wishes,' she retorted.

'I certainly would. That's the least I could do for him, and that's how much I care about my brother.' He ushered her along the path.

Remaining silent as they continued, her thoughts whirled round her mind until he cut in on them.

'Have you lost your tongue now?' he asked.

'Far from it,' she responded briskly. 'When I see Alex I shall tell him how you've acted.'

'If you cause any unpleasantness between us it will be Alex who suffers in the long run,' he warned.

'So you'd stoop to blackmail!' She looked at him angrily. 'Well, that's all I need to know! Don't expect me to fight fair after this.' She twisted away from him, and hurried back the way they had come.

At first she thought he would pursue her, and dared not pause until she was too breathless to run any farther. She had to stop eventually and looked around for him, only to experience disappointment because he had let her go.

She returned to the house, her thoughts in disarray and her mind confused by conflicting emotions.

She went to bed later, more tired than she cared to admit, hopeful that the morning would bring clarity to what now seemed like utter confusion. Her last thoughts, as she drifted into slumber, were of Adam kicking all of her lifelong attitudes to pieces, tearing down her carefully prepared defences, making nonsense of her values and arousing her feelings to fever pitch.

5

Cassie didn't see Adam the next morning when she arose. Thankful that she was feeling none the worse for her fall, she went down to breakfast with only the bump on her forehead to show for the accident.

Martha reported that Alex had left early and wouldn't be back until evening, and Cassie was relieved, for there was a growing insistence in her mind that compelled her to seek peace and solitude'.

She spent the morning in the garden, sitting in the shade, then reading and relaxing. In the afternoon, she went back to the beach for a swim. By the early evening she was feeling mentally refreshed, and was sitting at the dressing-table with just a dressing-gown on when a knock at the door startled her.

'Come in!' she called, expecting Martha to appear, or possibly Alex. She was slightly taken aback when Adam appeared.

'Hello,' he greeted with an unusual degree of friendliness in his tone. 'How are you feeling today? I heard that you've been resting. Are you better? No ill effects from the fall, I hope.'

'I'm fine, thank you.' She was aware that her heartbeats had quickened at the sight of him.

'I've just seen Alex,' he commented. 'He's going out on business this evening and leaving you alone again.'

'That's all right!' she exclaimed. 'What's wrong with that? Doesn't it show that we are prepared to take each other's pursuits seriously?'

'I wouldn't go off like that and leave my fiancée to moon about, especially when she's supposed to be on holiday.'

'Well you don't have a fiancée so you really don't know just how you would react, do you?' She paused. 'Anyway, I'm not exactly mooning about the place.'

'You don't have to get prickly with me just because Alex is going off on his own tonight!' he retorted.

Cassie felt anger rising but he smiled to defuse the situation.

'I'm teasing you,' he confessed. 'And you ought to see your face! You look ready to explode. But, whatever the reason Alex is going off tonight, I don't think it's right, so I've come to invite you to a function later on.

'It will be quite dreary, I warn you. I had arranged to take a girl but she called earlier to say that she is unwell. So would you give me the pleasure of your company?'

'What time would we leave?' Cassie fought down the eagerness which flared in her mind and forced her tone to remain calm.

'About seven-thirty.'

'H'm!' She glanced at her watch. 'That gives me time enough to get ready. If it will get you out of a spot, all right, I'll go. After all, I must try to help my future in-laws where possible. I never know when I may need a favour in return.'

'Look, if it will be too much of a chore then don't bother!' he told her.

'What's wrong?' She smiled. 'Does it upset you because I'm not exactly falling over myself to accompany you?'

'It doesn't really matter to me one way or another!' he told her. 'Just be ready at seven-thirty, if you would like to go.' He got up and strode to the door, shoulders stiff, and Cassie couldn't prevent herself from smiling.

*   *   *

At seven-thirty she was still in her room, although she was on the point of going down to locate Adam. She had dressed carefully for the occasion — a white off-the-shoulder dress with matching accessories, and was putting the finishing touches to her hair when there was a knock at the door and Adam opened it.

He was immaculate in a white evening jacket and black trousers. She caught her breath as she gazed at him.

'Time to go,' he said casually.

'I haven't really decided if I want to,' she countered, wanting to tease him a little more.

'I can give you a few more minutes in which to make up your mind, if you wish.'

His brown eyes regarded her steadily, as if he realised what she was doing. There was an inflexibility about him that was a little frightening, she thought. He seemed so self-assured, as if he knew all the answers and a few more beside.

She smiled inwardly, pleased because Alex was fooling him, and she wished that she could be on hand at the moment of revelation, when Alex finally explained the true situation.

'I'll go with you,' she said quietly, turning to pick up her handbag. She walked to the door, chin up, and found it difficult to conceal her pleasure.

He stepped aside and she preceded him down the stairs, keenly aware of his nearness. He escorted her out to his car and settled her in the front passenger seat. She watched him as he walked around the car to get in behind the steering wheel.

She felt comfortably relaxed and happy as he drove into town, where he pulled into a car park behind an imposing, two-storey building that was set on a cliff overlooking the bay. A score of cars were already parked, and Cassie wondered what kind of function they were attending. Adam's face was expressionless, so she made no comment as he locked the car and led her into the building.

There was a long dining-room set out for the function, and a crowded bar to the left was humming with chatter. The moment they walked through the doorway, Cassie was caught up in a merry-go-round of introductions.

Men and women were present in

equal numbers, apparently mostly married couples, and Adam, after procuring a drink for Cassie, inserted her into the company of several couples, then apologised and withdrew for a few moments.

Cassie sipped her drink and chatted animatedly to the woman nearest her, until a man's voice spoke at her side and she turned to see a tanned face smiling.

'Hello, Miss Overton,' the man greeted. 'I'm Pierre Marchant, Simone's father. I drove you home after your fall yesterday, but you were in no condition for us to be formally introduced. I didn't know Alex was bringing you here this evening.'

'How do you do, Mr Marchant?' she responded, and smiled. 'Alex didn't bring me. I'm with Adam.' She wondered if Simone was accompanying her father, and had decided that the woman wasn't the type to attend such a function when she spotted Simone across the room, talking to a man she could not quite see. Then a tall man who was masking her view moved away and she saw that Simone's companion was Adam himself.

'That's surprising,' Pierre said smoothly.

'What is?' Cassie countered.

'You being here with Adam.'

'Not at all. It's a family duty, apparently.' Cassie's attention was focused upon the two across the room. She saw Simone glancing around, as if looking for Cassie's position.

Pierre chuckled. 'I can understand Adam's problems, for I'm a widower so I usually have to bring Simone with me, and she hates it. When she sees you here with Adam I expect she will become quite disconsolate.'

Cassie glanced at him, wondering just how well he knew his daughter. 'Adam is talking to Simone now,' she observed.

'Ah! You will excuse me?' He smiled and moved away adroitly through the crowd.

Cassie wasn't left alone long. Adam

soon returned to her side.

'We can take our seats in the dining-room now,' he said. 'Come along.'

He led her along by the tables to the place marked with his name, seated her, then sat down opposite her. They were on the top table of the assembly, and again she wondered what the function was in aid of.

He seemed to read her mind because he leaned towards her. 'This is a meeting of the local chamber of commerce,' he explained. 'We have a large membership and these meetings are held every six weeks. I usually miss one in three, although it's in our own interests to attend when we can. Everybody who is anybody on the island is usually here, and even Tobias would have come had he felt well enough.'

'Does Alex ever attend?' she asked.

'As far as I know, never!' He smiled faintly, as if the thought of Alex mixing with *bona fide* businessfolk was too ludicrous for words.

Waiters began serving the meal and order arose from the apparent confusion that had attended their arrival. The food was good, the wine excellent, and Cassie enjoyed herself for the first time since arriving on the island.

She felt quite satisfied as the evening progressed. There were a number of speeches, but she listened with only half her attention, content to watch Adam's expression as he took in what was being said.

He was one of the most attractive men she had ever met, she told herself, noting the way his hair curled at the temples. When the power of her gaze attracted his eyes, he smiled faintly at her.

Then his name was called, and Cassie was surprised when he stood up and began to talk on business methods and what should be done to make more use of the natural resources of the island. He made a lot of sense, she realised, and clapped as loudly as the rest when he sat down.

Afterwards they retired to the bar, but after a couple of drinks, Adam ushered her out to the car, leaving Cassie feeling a little disappointed that the evening had come to an end.

He drove through the town instead of returning to the house, and when they pulled into an underground garage, he parked the car and turned to her.

'It's too early to go home yet,' he commented. 'The night life here sometimes leaves a lot to be desired, but there is a night club above us and it does provide a welcome diversion from the usual round. Would you like to go up or have you had enough of me for one evening?'

'You brought me here so I expect you are keen to visit,' she responded. 'I wouldn't want to spoil your evening, so let's go up.' Getting out of the car, Cassie was pleased at her cool reply. For once, in Adam's company, she'd been the one in command of the situation.

An elevator conveyed them to the upper floor where the club was situated, and when they left the elevator they were immediately caught up in local night life.

Cassie soon found herself installed in a lounge with a drink at hand and Adam sitting across from her. A female singer was rendering a ballad, and the big room was hazy with cigarette smoke.

Cassie soon began to feel the effects of the smoke and leaned towards Adam to complain.

He glanced around then nodded. 'It's pretty bad,' he admitted. 'If you would rather leave, I'll take you home, or we could visit the Mayfield yacht.'

'The yacht sounds interesting, if I have a choice,' she answered calmly.

'Come on then, let's go down to the waterfront,' he said. 'If you're not in a holiday mood at the moment I can soon put you in one. If Alex can't take the trouble to look after you then it's up to another Mayfield to do so.'

'Some more of that family duty you were talking about?' she asked, and saw him frown for a moment.

He escorted her from the club and they drove to the waterfront.

Cassie took the opportunity to study his face again. He glanced at her but didn't speak, and when he had parked on the quay he motioned toward the bay, now sparkling under a big tropical moon.

'There's the background scenery,' he said. 'Now all you need is the right man to make the romantic side of it come true.' He paused as she looked around, obviously entranced by the sheer beauty of the scene, then added, 'Alex is not the man for you, Cassie.'

There was a softness in his voice which she hadn't heard before, and it startled her as she looked at him. He was regarding her seriously.

'I don't want to fight with you tonight, Adam,' she said firmly. 'Why did you pick on me the moment I arrived? I'm not responsible for the way

Alex behaves. I've only known him five months and if anything, I restrained him slightly, which must be to the good. You asked me to help you with him but you must know that he will do his own thing, regardless.'

He alighted from the car without replying, then opened the passenger seat door to help her out.

'You're a strange woman,' he commented, guiding her to a wooden jetty, and for a few moments she had to concentrate on her feet as they negotiated a flight of shadowed wooden steps.

Adam sprang on to the sloping bows of a moored speedboat, then turned and held out both hands.

'Come on,' he invited. 'I won't let you fall into the water.'

'I'm not afraid of the water,' she declared, and stepped forward, almost taking him by surprise. She collided with him in stepping on to the boat and his arms instinctively whipped around her, drawing her close to his chest as the boat rocked wildly.

'Steady,' he warned. 'If I'm to go into the water I want to be wearing nothing but a pair of swimming trunks, not my best evening suit.'

His mouth was close to her ear, and he didn't release her, but moved slightly, so that he could see her face. The next instant his lips brushed her cheeks then lightly touched her lips.

She caught her breath, clinging to him as the boat tilted unexpectedly. Water gurgled between the craft and the jetty, and silver magic danced across the ripples of the bay.

'Sit down in the stern,' he said quietly, moving backwards and guiding her into the open cockpit. She made herself comfortable, watching intently as he cast off then started the engine. There was a throbbing cough, a powerful roar, and the craft shuddered from stem to stern.

Cassie grasped the side with a nervous hand, over-awed by so much power.

Adam sent the boat speeding across the bay. The water was calm and they soon reached top speed.

Cassie's heart thudded with sheer exhilaration. This seemed like the materialisation of an impossible dream and she wanted it never to end. When they had crossed the bay, Adam turned about, and eventually eased in beside a darkened sea-going yacht that was moored well out from the waterfront.

'Just stay put a moment.' He tied up to a landing stage. 'I'll put some lights on.' He ascended the steps that led to the deck and vanished, a mere shadow in the surrounding gloom.

Cassie glanced around appreciatively. There was a silver pathway across the water to the horizon where the moonlight dappled the gentle swell. Phosphorescence flickered eerily. A scented breeze blew gently into her face and she breathed deeply, wanting to retain a memory of this moment for ever.

Then, with breathtaking suddenness,

lights sprang into being all over the yacht. The rails were festooned with coloured lights, and a string of white globes between the masts cascaded stark brilliance upon the white-scrubbed deck.

Adam appeared at the rail, his handsome face merely a pale oval. He came down to the speedboat and reached out to take hold of Cassie's hand as she moved toward him.

He led her down to the saloon, and Cassie glanced around in delight. It was the last word in comfort; highly polished woodwork, carpets, and well upholstered furniture. He noted her expression and smiled as he moved to a cabinet, where he paused to switch on a stereo unit. The throbbing beat of music filled the saloon as Cassie sank into an easy chair.

He came to her side, handed her a drink then sat down on the arm of the chair with his own.

'Now you're supposed to get into a holiday mood,' he said.

'It hasn't been much of a holiday to

date,' she countered, shaking her head.

A strange nervousness was beginning to take hold of her. She moistened her lips, suddenly at a loss for words. She could only watch him, and ponder the strange magnetism he seemed to possess. No wonder Simone lost her head over him, she thought.

'I wouldn't like to see you get hurt in any way,' he said thoughtfully, sipping his drink. 'You shouldn't place too much faith in Alex, you know.'

'Poor Alex!' She looked up at him. 'Do you know that he hasn't said one nasty thing about you? But you knock him at every opportunity.'

'I speak the truth,' he told her, smiling. 'If you have stars in your eyes where Alex is concerned then you're not likely to observe any of his faults, so you should be warned.

'I know the general type of girl that Alex goes for,' he continued, 'and up until now not one of them has been worth a second glance. When you arrived you didn't act as if you were in love with him, so I assumed that you were out for what you could get.'

She shook her head. 'Your problem is that you're too arrogant for your own good. Do you think anyone really cares what you think about anything? And what if I was trying to get what I could out of Alex? Wouldn't it be better to let him find out for himself and gain valuable experience?' She gazed at him, trying to decide whether or not he was being deliberately offensive in the hope that she could be diverted from marrying into his family. 'There must be something wrong with Simone's good sense if she is in love with you!'

'Simone?' He frowned. 'How did she get into this?'

'When I first arrived she warned me off you, despite the fact that I am engaged to Alex.'

'What utter nonsense!' He stared frowningly at her, and she could sense his anger. He drained his glass before setting it down on a small table and, surprisingly, when he looked at her again he was smiling faintly.

'We seem to have developed an unfortunate knack of rubbing each other up the wrong way,' he observed. 'Now what do you suppose that is a sign of?'

She sipped her drink, ignoring the steady build-up of tension. Looking into his face, she met the power of his brown eyes and couldn't look away again.

He reached out with great deliberation, took the glass from her hand and set it down somewhere out of reach without looking or fumbling. She caught her breath as he cupped her chin in one hand. He stroked her cheek and heat suffused her face, then he brushed his lips against her mouth.

A tiny voice in her mind protested against his action because, as far as he knew, she was engaged to his brother but she revelled in the magic he aroused with his caress.

He drew her slowly into his embrace, his lips finding hers.

Cassie couldn't have resisted if she'd tried. She slid her arms around his neck. Excitement filled her until she feared that the intensity might completely overwhelm her.

He picked her up bodily and carried her across to a long divan by the far wall. Placing her gently upon it, he crouched and held her, his insistent fingers stroking her neck and shoulders. She uttered a little moan of delight when he bent his head and touched the curve of her throat with his lips.

Cassie could feel her resistance melting away as a wild abandonment began to seize hold of her. She closed her eyes, and even her hearing seemed to fade as the heady delight of pure ecstasy filled her.

Suddenly he drew back and when she opened her eyes he was regarding her steadily. 'Can you still say that you love Alex?' he asked.

She caught her breath and clutched at the last vestiges of her vanishing control. The import of his words struck her and she stiffened, bewildered by the conflict of emotions torturing her.

'You devil!' she cried, sitting up. 'So that's what you're trying to do! You'd compromise me and tell Alex in the hope that he'll send me packing. You don't give a damn about people or their emotions, do you?'

He smiled fleetingly before his expression hardened. 'All I know is that you are not in love with Alex!' he said harshly. 'Nor have you ever been! If you cared one scrap about him you would have complained the first time I kissed you but you were willing to let me carry on. Well that tells me a lot about you, Miss Cassandra Overton!'

She struggled to her feet. 'You're insufferable!' she shouted. 'I've had enough of this! Please take me home!' She fought down her anger and disappointment. 'I can't understand why you're putting pressure on me when it's Alex you should be talking to.'

Adam shrugged and rose to his feet and escorted her to the speedboat, taking great care to settle her in it safely. He left her then while he turned out the lights. When he rejoined her he glanced at her in the moonlight but she looked away, and he started the engine and unfastened the mooring rope.

During the trip back to the quay, Cassie realised that it would be impossible to find any happiness on this holiday, and wondered if her next move should be the return trip to England. Being the businesswoman that she was, it seemed the right time to cut her losses. All she could really hope to do was try to forget this most unfortunate episode in her life . . .

6

Cassie found however, during the ensuing week, that life settled into a smoother pattern. Time itself simply sped away, and days followed one another swiftly into oblivion. During that week she didn't once go out with Alex, for all his available time was taken up with other activities.

She came into contact more with Adam, who always seemed to be within arm's reach, as if he watched her movements and was determined to confront her.

Adam disappeared on an unexpected business trip the following week and didn't return until the following Sunday. Consequently, the days were less disrupted, and she filled in the time swimming or sight-seeing, having to be content with her own company.

She also had long chats with Tobias,

who proved to be perceptive and kind-hearted but she missed Adam's presence, and the night before he was due to return she was unable to sleep.

What really bothered her was the dawning realisation that Adam attracted her, that, against her will she was drifting helplessly into the stormy waters of love!

The next morning, she went into the kitchen for breakfast, and learned from Martha that Adam had returned during the night but Alex wasn't at home, having telephoned to say that he was making a trip to a neighbouring island.

Cassie ate her breakfast, and afterwards took a buggy down to the beach. She swam a little before stretching out in the sun, and the heat that blazed down from the brilliant sky lulled her to the point of slumber, until she heard thudding hooves rapidly approaching.

Looking around quickly, she saw Adam approaching, and her heart seemed to leap disconcertingly as he drew nearer and she could see his face.

He dismounted and came over, looking rather grim.

'What's wrong?' she asked.

'Tobias collapsed this morning. He's been put to bed and the doctor says he must stay there until further orders.' He paused, his expression showing strain. 'I need to know where Alex is.'

'I don't know his whereabouts,' she confessed. 'He didn't tell me where he was going.'

'What a pair you are! This could be a matter of life and death!' He stared at her for a moment, dark eyes filled with a harsh light then he turned and sprang back into his saddle. The next instant he was galloping back the way he had come.

Cassie watched until he was out of sight, then she folded the towel. After changing in the beach house, she started the drive back to the house.

It was gloomy under the trees and she travelled slowly on the uphill stretches. Reaching an awkward bend where, on her left, the track almost disappeared on the edge of a deep ravine, she changed gear and began to negotiate it.

At that instant an ominous crackling sound became apparent, startling her with its loudness. She glanced at the slope on her right and was shocked to see a stack of huge felled logs breaking loose at the top. Already they were crashing and rumbling towards her!

Cassie was horror-stricken and, unable to do anything but continue to steer the buggy around the bend, she accelerated instinctively but only succeeded in pushing the vehicle outwards to the edge of the precipice. She changed her mind instantly and slammed on the brakes, bringing the vehicle to a halt exactly in the path of the tumbling logs.

Without thinking, she jumped out of the vehicle and threw herself against the inside of the path, where she crouched under an overhanging rock. A split second later the first of the heavy logs crashed overhead, shot off the top of her cover and plummeted down the precipice to splinter in the ravine far below.

Seconds later the main bulk of logs struck the buggy and carried it off the path and into the ravine. Cassie remained crouched in timeless horror. The noise of the moving logs filled her with paralysing fear as dust rose in a billowing cloud. Then silence returned, and she began to stir.

Leaving the shelter of the rock, she realised that if she hadn't taken cover she would now be dead. Then reaction caught her and she trembled uncontrollably. She staggered away from the grim spot, filled with a haunting fear. The only thing that stood out clearly in her mind was the fact that her holiday, such as it had been, now seemed to be well and truly over. The grim incident had shocked her into stark reality.

She was about two miles from the house, and there was nothing for it but to walk. Cassie felt tired and weak and when she emerged from the trees a great heat seared her shoulders. Her head ached and shock enveloped her thoughts. She knew she'd never forget what had just happened.

It took her more than an hour to get within sight of the house. The knowledge that she had been close to death was numbing, and she had to fight against an urge to break down and weep. She went forward step by weary step until she reached the terrace and, as she crossed it thankfully, Alex appeared at the french windows leading into the library.

Cassie almost collapsed when she saw him.

'What on earth happened to you, Cassie?' he cried, hurrying to her side.

'Adam was looking for you,' she countered dazedly.

'Never mind Adam! You're covered in dust. Cassie — have you had an accident?'

'I'm afraid the buggy is smashed.' She shook her head, fighting against the sickening horror which nearly overwhelmed her. Her senses wavered and there was a buzzing in her ears.

She was only dimly aware of being carried into the library and placed on a couch. The next moment her head was raised and brandy trickled between her lips. She choked and spluttered as it burned her throat.

'Take it easy,' Alex soothed. 'You're safe now. Just tell me what happened.'

At that moment there was a flicker of movement in the doorway, and she looked up to see Adam standing there.

Alex noted her change of expression and glanced over his shoulder.

'Where the devil have you been, Alex?' Adam demanded, coming into the room.

'I don't like your tone,' Alex responded, getting to his feet. 'What's so important about my presence here? No one has ever worried about me in the past.'

'You have a duty to be here.' Adam's keen gaze was upon Cassie. 'It's about time you began facing up to your responsibilities.'

'I'm doing just that, and we'll

certainly discuss it later. But right now I'm trying to find out what happened to Cassie. Something's happened, but she doesn't want to talk about it.' There was a new firmness in Alex's voice.

'Cassie?' Adam frowned as he transferred his gaze to her. 'What's wrong?'

'She said something about the buggy being smashed.' Alex returned his attention to Cassie. 'Did you have an accident?' he asked again.

Cassie fought to overcome the shock that still gripped her, and began to explain what had happened. She saw them exchange glances before her narrative ended, but they continued to listen in silence until she finished, then Adam came to her side and looked intently into her eyes.

'Were you hurt at all?' he asked.

'No,' she held her breath for a moment, 'just really frightened and shocked.'

Adam sighed heavily and shook his head. 'I'll go and check out the spot,' he said harshly, turning on his heel. 'Those logs should never have been stacked at the top of that slope.' As he reached the door his brother spoke again.

'At least you can't blame me for that,' Alex said.

'Perhaps not, but if you had been here, pulling your weight, I'd have had more time to check what's going on around the place,' Adam snapped, before turning and departing.

Cassie stood up, shivering despite the heat.

Alex took hold of her hand. 'Are you sure you're all right? You look awfully pale.'

'I'll be fine,' she assured him. 'It was quite a shock, believe me, but give me a little time and I'll get over it. I'll shower and change then go and see Tobias. But this little episode has put my mind into focus, Alex. I don't think I can go on with this charade any longer. It looks as if the best thing I can do is return to England. You certainly started a bad situation when you said we were engaged to be married.'

'I've regretted it myself,' he admitted. 'But, having told the lie, we're now stuck with it. Grandfather is in no condition to withstand another shock. I'm sorry, Cassie. I know you really needed this holiday. Look, why don't you put off a decision for a few days? Let's see how things turn out.'

'Only if you promise to tell Adam the truth about us,' she said firmly.

'All right, I promise,' he agreed instantly, and smiled. 'Will you manage to get to your room?' he asked then.

She nodded and walked unsteadily to the door, and, despite the shock still gripping her, realised that at last she had made some progress where Alex was concerned. But what she really wanted was to see Adam's face when he learned the truth! He had practically accused her of scheming to marry into the Mayfield family for money, and it would give her great satisfaction to have him admit that he was wrong, and perhaps apologise to her.

After showering and changing her

clothes, Cassie felt almost her old self, but when she peeped into Tobias's room he was sleeping soundly, so she went down to the kitchen to sit on the back porch with Martha.

About thirty minutes later a buggy appeared round a corner and came screeching to a halt in front of the porch. Cassie suppressed a shiver at the sight of it, and caught her breath as Adam alighted and came striding purposefully towards her.

'How are you feeling now?' he asked, pausing on the bottom step and subjecting her to a scrutiny that brought colour to her cheeks. 'Are you sure you weren't hurt?'

'Quite sure. I was just badly shaken, that's all.'

'From what I saw of the spot, it's a miracle you weren't killed!'

Martha got to her feet and turned to the kitchen. 'I'll get you a cold drink, Masta Adam,' she said woodenly, as if she held Adam to blame for the incident.

Adam stood looking down into Cassie's face. His brown eyes were narrowed, his expression harsh. For a moment he was stiffly motionless, then he relaxed, and mounted the porch steps to sit down in the seat that Martha had vacated. He leaned across and placed a hand on Cassie's arm.

'I'm sorry about the accident,' he said. 'It's been in the back of my mind ever since the logs were stacked that it could be a dangerous place to leave them, but I've been so busy I'd forgotten. However, if no harm has been done then I've been let off extremely lightly.'

'I'm the one who got off lightly,' Cassie responded, conscious of his hand upon her. 'But you've lost a buggy.'

'Thank Heaven it was only the buggy. I think that's a small price to pay for having you come through it unscathed, don't you?' His hand tightened convulsively upon her arm. 'Are you sure you're all right? Shall I call Doctor Stephenson?'

'No, thank you. I'm fine, honestly.' Adam's touch was sending shivers along her spine, but he suddenly released her.

'That's a relief,' he spoke, then his expression changed. 'Now I must talk to Alex,' he said firmly. 'Where is he, do you know?'

'He drove into town about thirty minutes ago,' Martha informed him as she emerged from the kitchen with a tray of cold drinks.

'After what's happened?' Adam spoke angrily. 'You are his responsibility, Cassie, and he'd better start facing up to reality before something happens that he may live to regret.'

'What else could happen?' Cassie asked wryly.

Adam shook his head, took a can of cold beer from the tray, and departed without replying.

Cassie's head was aching. Her emotions were in turmoil. She was in love with Adam! The knowledge was stark in her mind but the situation was impossible and she couldn't see any way out of it.

She spent the rest of the day close to the house, content to relax and recover from the shock of the incident.

Alex returned late in the afternoon, but did no more than change into a suit, have a cold beer, and depart once more.

Cassie didn't even bother to try to engage him in conversation. Instead, she rested on the terrace, feeling strangely exhausted.

★　★　★

It was early evening when Adam reappeared. He came into the library, where Cassie was sitting reading, and poured himself a drink. He seemed harassed, and merely glanced at her before slumping into a big easy chair and gulping his drink.

'You look as if you've been busy,' she observed, for the sake of breaking the silence.

'I'm always busy. I usually do the work of two men.'

'Your own and Alex's?'

He gazed at her as if suspecting sarcasm behind her words. His gaze was most disturbing, Cassie discovered, and wondered what was going on in his mind.

'I feel like a swim in the cove,' he said abruptly. 'Would you like to come?'

She stifled the instinct to agree immediately, and experienced a cold chill when thoughts of the accident returned. He must have seen her changing expression for he came across to her and placed a hand on her shoulder.

'There's nothing else along the road that could hurt you,' he assured her, 'so don't be afraid.'

'All right,' she agreed. 'I'd like to swim.'

'Good. See you in the kitchen in ten minutes.'

Later, when she entered the kitchen, carrying her swimsuit, Adam was there.

'The buggy is out back,' he said, taking his leave of Martha, and Cassie followed him out to the porch. She suppressed a shiver at the sight of the buggy, a replica of the one that had been swept into the ravine by the logs, and faltered until he took her arm and led her forward.

'You'll have to put that incident right out of your mind,' he told her quietly.

She didn't reply, and sat with her hands clasped together, remaining silent, as he drove smoothly along the track to the beach.

'I'll sit out here while you go in and change,' Adam said, when they arrived at the beach house. 'I'll go in when you've finished.'

Cassie nodded and went inside to change into her bikini and select a towel. When she went out to the buggy, Adam subjected her to a long, searching glance. She sat quietly in the buggy until he emerged from the beach house.

He was wearing a pair of black trunks, his bronzed body well-muscled and athletic — powerful shoulders, strong arms and a slim waist. Dark hair was clustered on his chest. Without clothes he didn't seem so formidable, she thought; looked human, in fact!

He saw her inspecting him and grinned boyishly as he slid behind the wheel of the buggy.

'Let's go and swim,' he commented, driving towards the shore. 'I've been waiting all day for this.'

Cassie mentally agreed, and wished that this particular moment would never end.

7

Cassie had no desire to enter the water when she finally stood on the shore but stretched out on a towel and sat down on it while Adam swam energetically.

She could hear him splashing, and firmly ignored his occasional commands to join him. She lay quietly, her limbs now adequately tanned, eyes closed and senses lulled by the swish of the waves.

In the background the booming roar of surf pounding the reef was strangely muted, and quite soothing. It was the first time she had been able to completely relax since the accident, and she didn't stir a muscle until Adam's feet pounded the hard white sand and he threw himself down full length at her side. Droplets of water splashed her, and he laughed when she opened her eyes and protested.

'Why didn't you come in?' he asked. Adam's dark hair was tousled and wet upon his forehead. His dark eyes glinted as they regarded her, boldly inspecting her figure.

She drew a defensive breath, began to tense, then forced herself to relax.

'You'll join me in there shortly,' he threatened, 'because I'll throw you in.'

'I suspected from the outset that you're a bully,' she retorted, smiling.

He was so close she could feel the fine hairs on his forearm tickling her shoulder, and his nearness drew her imperceptibly.

He turned on his side to face her, wiping a hand on his trunks. His fingers were pleasantly cool when he placed them on her shoulder.

'I've never bullied a woman in my life,' he replied, 'and I don't intend to start now.' A fingertip began tracing the line of her shoulder. 'So you're going to marry Alex, are you?'

Cassie was completely relaxed, her eyes closed, and she was determined not to reply. He believed she was engaged to Alex. The knowledge hurt her because he wasn't the kind of man she wanted if he couldn't keep his hands off his brother's future wife!

'Why don't you answer?' His tone was sharp. 'I know you're not in love with Alex. It's as plain as if it were written on your face. In fact it is written there! So why don't you admit it?'

His voice sounded very close and Cassie opened her eyes a little and peered at him. Her pulses were racing, and she fancied that he would hear the fast beating of her heart.

'All right,' he went on softly. 'Have it your way. But I am bound by family duty to see that you don't marry Alex if your only reason for so doing is the Mayfield money.'

'How many times do I have to tell you that I don't need the Mayfield money?' she responded, keeping her tone casual. 'You obviously don't know a thing about me, Adam, and I'm quite surprised that you haven't checked me out.'

'Well, I didn't.' He leaned closer, and she felt his warm breath on her neck. 'But only because Tobias knows all about your family.' He leaned even closer. His forearm touched her stomach and his chest pressed more heavily against her shoulder. The next instant his lips brushed her cheek.

She caught her breath, engulfed by a surge of emotion, and turned her head slightly towards him.

'Ah!' he accused instantly. 'So much for you being in love with Alex.'

Cassie pushed him away and sat up, shaking sand out of her hair. She opened her eyes wide and gazed at him, her heart aching with love. She longed to push herself into the circle of his arms but fought down the urge and tried to contain her emotion as she spoke.

'Keep your distance then!' Her tone was harsher than she intended. 'You take your family duties far too seriously. I'm sure Alex wouldn't like to know that his twin brother is handling his future wife under the pretext of testing her fidelity!'

'He would thank me if I proved that she was not marrying for love!' He turned on his back and stretched out, putting his hands behind his head and interlacing his fingers. 'Nothing is ever simple in this life,' he complained softly, his eyes narrowed now.

Cassie watched him, her admiring gaze on his firm body. He was perfectly tanned which suggested that he did find some time to relax in the sun.

He attracted her, had done so from the very beginning, and it was a pity that Alex had placed insurmountable barriers between them. She would have liked to discover his real nature. At the moment he seemed more like an opportunist out to grasp what he could, regardless if she were morally his twin brother's property. But a future sister-in-law should be taboo, she thought dismally.

She wondered just how far he would

go, although she realised it would be dangerous to try to find out. Yet she would like to know whether there was real interest in him. But it would count for nothing if he responded while under the impression that she and Alex were engaged!

She stretched and arched her back, aware that his gaze was upon her, his brow furrowed but his eyes showing approval at what he saw.

'Look, I really need this holiday, or what's left of it,' she said seriously. 'I worked extremely hard all year back in England, and some of the toughest dealing I handled was with Alex when he was acting for your company. You must know all the details from your side so you'll understand what passed between us. Alex fought hard and you can be proud of him. He doesn't have much to learn about business, and you should now give him a full measure of responsibility.'

'Did you really handle Overton's side of the business for your father's company?' he asked in some surprise. 'I thought Alex was just trying to present you in a favourable light.'

'I certainly handled it.' She glanced at him. 'Why the surprise? Don't I look intelligent enough?'

'Of course you do. That's not what I'm getting at.' He shrugged off her question as infantile. 'Now I come to think of it, Alex mentioned, in the letter he wrote to Grandfather, something about the woman he was dealing with. He said she was a female replica of me and my business methods, which is a compliment to you, by the way. But now I recall he also said you were fifty, ugly as sin, and would make me a perfect wife! Just wait until I see him!'

'Is Alex always so flattering?' Cassie laughed. 'But do I see new respect for me in your eyes?'

'I certainly admire your business acumen after the trouble you gave us before we clinched the deal.' He spoke grudgingly. 'So you're a female whizz kid! Well, perhaps I can interest you in some business. There are endless opportunities out here.'

'For the next two weeks I don't want to hear a word of business, thank you,' she retorted.

'All right.' He smiled. 'I'll make a deal with you. Let's have a truce while you enjoy the rest of your holiday. But I'm not at all happy about Alex,' he added. 'It seems as if he's trying to make you unhappy instead of the other way around, and I still suspect him of trying to pull a fast one over Tobias.'

She eased away from him, smiling. 'I can't help you there, I'm afraid. Alex is a law unto himself, you know that.'

If only Adam had come to England five months ago instead of Alex, she thought.

'I know all about Alex,' he answered. 'But no man is a law unto himself.'

'Alex is,' she insisted.

'You don't know very much about the man you say you're going to marry!' He sat up, and glanced around. 'I think we'd better start back now,' he suggested, his tone strangely flat.

She felt disappointed as they changed and, when Adam drove back to the house, Cassie was thoughtful until they drew in beside the back porch. As he got out of the buggy she leaned over.

'I want to tell you that it's in the back of my mind to cut my holiday short and return to England,' she said, aware that subconsciously she was endeavouring to find a way to reveal to him the true situation, and yet realising that at the moment it was impossible to do so.

He stared at her, a frown between his eyes. 'That sounds as if you're considering leaving Alex,' he said at length. 'So you're not truly in love with him. If you were then nothing could make you leave.'

She considered his words, aware that leaving would mean she might never see him again, and that didn't appeal to her by any stretch of the imagination. But he didn't appear to be concerned that she might now depart from his life.

She wondered how he could kiss her the way he did and not feel something afterwards.

'I don't know what to do,' she confessed. 'Perhaps going home would be better for everyone concerned. Nothing seems to have gone right since my arrival.'

'If you went home, would that mean your engagement to Alex is off?' he demanded.

'You sound as if you'd be relieved!' She smiled wryly. 'Are you so scared that Alex might marry the wrong woman? You know you can't tell what kind of a girl I really am just by kissing me. I'm aware that you're merely testing me, and you should be wise to the fact that I might be playing up to you. So it's give and take, and you can't be any the wiser about me.'

He regarded her, smiling at little. 'I have a great many doubts about this situation Alex seems to have involved us in. In fact, the only thing I'm certain of is that he shouldn't have returned from

Europe at this time.'

'Because of your grandfather?'

'Tobias always figures prominently in my calculations, and that is one of the reasons why I haven't seriously considered marriage myself. A wife might want to live elsewhere in the world, and I have to be here to look after Tobias as well as the business.'

'You shouldn't tie yourself down like that,' she protested. 'It isn't fair. And I'll bet Tobias would have something to say about that if he knew.'

He shrugged and turned away, then glanced back at her. 'Thanks for going down to the cove with me,' he said. 'I really enjoyed it.'

'My pleasure,' she responded.

Going up to her room, Cassie showered then prepared to go to bed. She was physically and mentally exhausted by the events of the day.

She paused when there was a knock at the door, and pulled on a dressing-gown before going to answer. Expecting to see Adam, she was surprised to find Tobias outside.

'What on earth are you doing out of bed?' she asked, then added solicitously, 'How are you feeling now?'

'I'm fine. Are you available for a chat or are you about to go to bed? I can't sleep, and I heard you come in. I can never sleep at night when I've been forced to lie in bed all day. But tomorrow I'll get up, no matter what anyone says. I'm the best judge on how I feel.' He grimaced.

'Adam always had a tendency to coddle me because of my age,' Tobias continued. 'He means well, I've no doubt, but it's all so boring and unnecessary. I suppose he told you that I'd collapsed, or something?' His eyes twinkled. 'Well, there's nothing wrong with me.'

'Shall I come to your room for a chat?' she asked.

'No, let's go down to the library,' he suggested. 'Then I can have a drink.'

She followed as he led the way down the stairs, and he ushered her into the library and closed the door. He was wearing pyjamas and a dressing-gown, his feet pushed into comfortable slippers.

'Can I get you something?' he inquired, advancing upon the drinks cabinet.

'A sherry, please.' She glanced at the desk, imagining Adam sitting there.

Tobias poured drinks and handed one to her. She thanked him, her thoughts still upon Adam.

'You are not enjoying your holiday, are you?' he asked.

'No, not really.' She shook her head. 'And I was so looking forward to it.' She broke off and stared at him. 'But how do you know? You haven't seen me very often. I'm on the point of calling off my holiday and returning home,' she added.

'There's no need to do that.' He regarded her for a moment, and his hands shook slightly as he raised them. 'I'm too old to deal with the problems and worry I've had recently. You know,' he continued, 'it was good for me having to rear Adam and Alex after their parents died. Now I feel that they can stand on their own two feet at last, and tomorrow morning I'm going to tell them just that. They will have to take over the business! I'm going to London to live out the rest of my life peacefully.'

He held up a hand as Cassie opened her mouth to speak. 'No, please hear me out. I've made a big decision but I need to put it into words, and I want to hear what it sounds like before I tell it to my grandsons.'

She nodded, sipping her drink while he deliberated.

'I'm calling a halt to all the time-wasting and the play-boying. I'm now prepared to relinquish all control in the Mayfield companies. The younger generation will have to prove what it can do.'

'Adam can handle anything,' Cassie opined.

'That's right,' he agreed. 'I have no

doubts about that. But Alex has to start pulling his weight, and I plan to throw him in at the deep end! If he can swim then all well and good.' He paused and chuckled. 'And if he can't, then the experience should do him good.'

Cassie nodded soberly. Under the circumstances, she fancied that Tobias was doing the right thing. It was a pity, she thought dismally, that she would not be around to see the outcome!

8

Cassie slept poorly that night, her mind so active that she tossed and turned restlessly. She awoke early the next morning and arose with relief.

After showering, she dressed in shorts and a suntop, pushed her feet into sandals, and went down to the kitchen to get something to eat before setting out for a walk. She was still restless, and wanted exercise and fresh air. When she entered the kitchen and found it deserted she was pleased, because she didn't even feel like talking to Martha before she had the opportunity to do some straight thinking in solitude.

Before she had finished her cereal, footsteps sounded in the hall and she frowned when they paused at the kitchen door. She sat still. The footsteps were heavy, probably Alex and she didn't feel like talking to him at this time of the day.

He had tricked her into accepting this doubtful situation for the last time, and, after Tobias had talked to him, she would add her own rider. This was the day when Alex had to grow up and face life squarely.

After some hesitation the footsteps went on, and she felt relieved. When the front door closed she tip-toed into the hall and peered from a window to see Adam departing, and a frown marred her expression. She watched him follow the path that led to the garages, and a few moments later a car appeared then departed swiftly. She felt depressed.

'What are you doing up so early, Cassie?' Alex spoke quietly at her back, startling her, and she swung round to see him standing at the foot of the stairs. He was fully dressed and carrying a small case.

'Where are you going?' she countered.

He looked a bit sheepish as he

approached, and twice glanced at the stairs as if afraid that Tobias or Adam would appear.

'I have to make a trip. It's a bit unexpected, but very important.' He paused. 'Are you enjoying your holiday?'

She smiled and shook her head. Mindful of the fact that Tobias planned to talk to Alex on important issues, she knew that he had to be made aware of the changing situation.

'We'd better have a talk before you go anywhere,' she said firmly.

'I don't have the time right now.' He glanced at his watch. She had never seen him so decisive, and he reminded her of Adam. 'I've a plane to catch. I'll be away three days.'

'I'll go with you to the airport,' she decided instantly. 'I must talk with you, Alex.'

'Come along then.' He was frowning. 'You can bring the car back for me.'

Cassie followed him outside, and remained silent until they were driving toward the town. She glanced at him several times but his expression was closed, as if he had a lot on his mind and could not be prevailed upon to talk about it.

'May I ask where you're going and what you're planning?' she asked, at length, when she was certain that he wasn't going to talk voluntarily. 'We are friends, Alex, and, if nothing else, you can trust me.'

He thought for a moment then nodded. 'Of course,' he said slowly, and smiled at her. 'Well, I'll tell you if you promise to keep quiet until I get back.' He glanced at her and she raised an eyebrow, tacitly informing him that it would be a most unnecessary promise. 'I'm meeting Kirsty at the airport,' he said finally. 'We're going to the States to get married.'

'What? Then you'll come back and confront Tobias with your new wife while your ex-fiancée is still in the house?' Cassie was shocked. 'After all that talk about not upsetting Tobias!

You know what might happen if you do that, surely? But you'd do well to postpone your plans for a few days, Alex. A number of changes are about to overtake you and Adam.'

'I knew you'd say that!' He exhaled sharply. 'Nobody wants me to do what pleases me, and everybody has such plans for me. I wish I could do what I want just once without a lot of argument or so-called sound advice.'

'Tobias wants you to be happy,' Cassie said sharply. 'He's planning to speak to you and Adam this morning. There are big developments in the wind.' She gave him the gist of Tobias's intentions, and it was his turn to evince surprise.

'When did you talk to Tobias?' he asked.

'It was more his talking to me,' she retorted. 'Last night. Ordinarily I wouldn't betray his confidence, but if it will stop you making a wrong move at this time then I feel justified in doing so. If you don't heed this warning, Alex, you'll probably rue the decision for the rest of your life.'

He glanced at his watch again, and frowned. 'If what you say is true then I would certainly be making a big mistake by going ahead with my plans,' he mused. 'But I saw Adam drive away from the house just before I came down. Have you any idea where he went?'

'No.' She shook her head. 'He certainly doesn't confide in me, as you know. Please don't do anything rash, Alex.'

'I won't,' he answered thoughtfully. 'But I have to get a move on. I'll call off this trip then come home.'

'You can drop me off here,' she decided. 'I'll walk back.'

He brought the car to a halt, and put a hand on her arm as she opened the door to alight. 'Cassie, I want to tell you what a real friend you've been, and all I can say is thank you for everything. But that doesn't seem to cover it, you know, and I feel so guilty about your holiday.'

'What holiday?' she countered, and smiled to take the sting out of her words. 'Don't spare a thought for me, Alex,' she told him. 'I'm enjoying myself, really. You just go and do what's right, that's all I ask.'

He nodded, and there was a tender smile on his lips.

Cassie got out of the car and turned back the way they had come. She glanced over her shoulder as he drove on, and when the car had disappeared from view she continued at a brisk walk, her thoughts busy.

Her mind was inundated with conjecture as she strode along the road that crossed the fields. The sun was shining brilliantly despite the early hour, and the faint breeze had fire in its breath, a promise of what she could expect during the daylit hours.

This morning she was more positive of her feelings. She loved Adam, and nothing else mattered in the face of that knowledge. But it was an emotion that seemed doomed to an early demise.

Everything had conspired against them from the start, she realized, and it would be the sensible thing to forget that she'd ever met him. But the memory of his embraces stayed with her and he was in her thoughts constantly.

Where had Adam gone so early this morning? Despite the knowledge that she ought to forget about him, she was eager to see him again, and speculated on the site of the mill that Martha had so often mentioned, which seemed to demand so much of his time.

Thank goodness she was not engaged to Alex! Her thoughts moved in time with her feet as she strode along the dusty road, and she reviewed the situation without arriving at any decision until she heard a car approaching from behind. She threw a quick glance over her shoulder and immediately recognised the car as Adam's.

He was already braking, and raised dust as he pulled in beside her. He leaned across and opened the nearside door, and Cassie bent and peered in at him, aware that she was hot and dry and that the idea of taking a long walk was no longer a good one.

'What are you doing out here, in the middle of nowhere?' he demanded sharply, and her smile faded. 'I saw Alex driving like a maniac to town. Did you start out with him?'

'Yes.' She froze a little at his tone.

'And he dropped you off out here?'

'I wanted to walk back to the house.'

'Why? Did you two have an argument?'

'No, we didn't!' She shook her head, and couldn't resist saying, 'And you needn't sound so hopeful.'

He didn't smile and she mentally withdrew. 'I'll carry on walking,' she said sharply, and turned and strode off.

He drove the car just ahead of her and stopped again. The nearside door was opened again and he slid across and emerged just as she reached him.

'You can't walk all that way,' he told

her. 'Get into the car and I'll drive you home.'

'Thank you, but I prefer to walk,' she replied, perversely.

'I'll drive us home and then we'll take a walk together, if you must walk,' he insisted. 'But you're not properly attired for a long period in the sun. Alex must be mad to bring you out like that.'

'You don't seem to be in the mood for company, especially mine,' she flung at him. 'Did you get out of bed on the wrong side this morning?'

He frowned. 'Just because you and Alex have had a difference of opinion you don't have to take it out on me!' he retorted. 'I suppose you asked him to take you somewhere but he's gone off to do whatever has occupied him every day since his return. If he put as much effort into his attempts at business as he does into his pleasures then he would become highly successful.'

'There's nothing the matter with me,' she insisted. 'You're the one who sounds grumpy. You looked bad-tempered when you first stopped the car. If you're in a bad humour then drive on. I'm quite happy to walk alone.'

'Oh, get into the car and don't make every day a pitched battle,' he snapped. 'I've enough on my mind without you adding to it!'

'Me!' She turned to start walking again, but he grasped her arm and held on when she began to struggle. 'You're the very limit!' she told him.

'Don't blame me because your romance with Alex is turning sour!' He glared at her. 'I knew it would! I tried to warn you but you wouldn't listen. You had to find out the hard way, didn't you? So all right, go ahead and suffer, but just remember that I told you so!'

She stopped resisting him and turned back to the car, aware that he wouldn't let her go on alone.

Adam's face was set in harsh lines as he drove on in silence. He didn't speak again until they reached the house.

'What are your plans for today?' he asked. 'Have you made any?'

176

'That's no concern of yours.' She folded her arms and gazed moodily through the windscreen.

'So now you're sulking! That's all I need!' He stopped the car at the terrace.

Cassie alighted quickly, wanting to get away from him, and hurried into the house, where she met Tobias, who was walking to the door.

'Hello,' he greeted. 'You're moving fast for this time of the day.'

'Good morning, Tobias,' she responded and at that moment, Adam came bounding into the house in pursuit and collided with her. She was thrust forward by the impact and found herself in Tobias's arms.

'What it is to be young!' Tobias murmured. 'Adam, I want to talk to you.'

'Later, Grandfather,' Adam responded testily. 'There's something I have to discuss with Cassie.'

'It looked as if she was running away from you,' Tobias told him, glancing questioningly at Cassie. 'But I'm afraid your personal affairs will have to wait. I have something of great importance to discuss with you.'

'I'm going up to my room,' Cassie said, and moved toward the stairs.

'Not until I've spoken to you,' Adam rapped, following her.

'You'll have the rest of the day to play childish games,' Tobias protested. 'Adam, pay attention! Get Alex and bring him into the library. This is the day I retire from business. I'm going to make arrangements to move to England. Also, I want to be gone from here by the end of the month.'

Adam stopped, looking round in surprise as he took in the importance of Tobias's words. He stared at his grandfather.

Cassie studied his features, told herself that she loved him, and walked up the stairs to her room.

Behind her, Adam began plying Tobias with questions and Cassie smiled wryly. As usual, business was taking precedence over everything else!

★ ★ ★

Cassie was still in her room later when there was a tap at the door. She hoped in a way it wasn't Adam because she didn't feel like continuing the argument they had begun earlier. However, it was Alex who came into the room.

'Hello,' he greeted her cheerfully. 'I want to thank you for putting me right this morning. I've just left Tobias, and it's a good thing I didn't go ahead with my plans. Mind you, it took a lot of explaining to convince Kirsty that I wasn't making excuses to back out, but she's an understanding woman, thank goodness. Things are really moving now,' he added.

'I'm glad.' Cassie smiled. 'So now everyone knows that we were never engaged?'

'No!' He frowned. 'I was going to bring that into the open, honestly, but the opportunity never arose. When I did broach the subject, Tobias was in the process of repeating himself and cut me

179

out! I'm sorry, Cassie, but it's easier to let the situation stand for the moment.'

'The situation is ridiculous!' Cassie said angrily. 'I can't go on like this! If I had any sense at all I'd cancel this travesty of a holiday and go home. I've threatened to do so before but I let you talk me out of it. Now I think I ought to cut my losses. It's obvious matters will never improve.'

'I'm sorry,' Alex spoke quietly. 'And I have to tell you that when I left Tobias, Adam was waiting for me in the hall and almost dragged me into the drawing-room to talk. He said that if I had any sense at all I'd break off our engagement. He's certain you're not the girl for me, and said that if I married you it would be courting disaster.' He sighed. 'I can't understand why Adam should get so uptight about us.'

'Did he really say that?' Cassie was horrified.

Alex nodded.

'Well, that's all I need,' she retorted.

'Thanks for telling me, Alex. You've done something right for a change. Now will you do something for me?'

'Just name it,' he said readily.

'Book me a seat on the first available flight to London, please.'

He stared at her for a moment, trying to gauge her mood, then nodded. 'All right, Cassie, just leave it to me.' He patted her arm and turned away. 'It won't be before tomorrow, you know.'

'That's all right. If you'll just go ahead and do it. I'll start packing today,' she added.

'You'd better tell Tobias that you're leaving,' he suggested from the doorway.

'I'll take care of that shortly,' she promised.

Alex departed and she considered her prospects. So Adam had finally spoken to Alex about her. He still didn't know that no engagement existed, but he had made his feelings toward her quite plain. He had advised Alex against marrying her. She smiled wryly, trying to drag her thoughts from the subject. Well, it didn't matter any more. She was going home tomorrow.

Later, as she was going down the stairs, Adam emerged from the kitchen, and paused at the foot of the stairs when he saw her. His face was showing displeasure.

'I have some good news for you,' she said brightly, smiling to show that she wasn't hurt, although her heart felt as if it had been cut in two. 'I'm going back to London tomorrow.'

His face didn't change expression and a pang of disappointment ached through her. He didn't seem to be the least bit concerned by the fact that he would never see her again after tomorrow. But then he had never shown an interest in her beyond the physical testing of her attitude. She had fallen in love with him but he had remained untouched by her presence.

'What about your engagement to Alex?' he demanded.

'I'll leave you to tell him that it is off.'

She smiled. 'That should make your day! You've tried hard enough to break us up.'

'I must admit that I am relieved your plans to marry Alex have fallen through,' he replied quietly. 'Have you made your plane reservation?'

'Alex is taking care of that for me.' She fought against tears. He even had the nerve to admit being relieved by the turn of events.

'I wouldn't trust Alex to get that right.' He smiled. 'I'll check that it has been done.' He turned away, but paused as if a thought had suddenly come to him. 'Tonight we're going into town to celebrate Tobias's retirement and our taking over the company. Tobias would like you to be there.'

'Certainly!' Her eyes were overbright as she smiled to him. 'It doesn't matter how I fill in my last hours here.'

He stared bleakly at her. 'Fine. Well, if you could be ready by about seven this evening. We'll probably leave about then.'

She nodded and he turned away and went out of the house.

In the kitchen, Martha was singing in a shrill voice, and Cassie, overwhelmed, turned to flee to the sanctuary of her room.

9

It didn't take Cassie long to pack, and, as they were going to dine out later, she felt no desire to eat before evening. She checked that nothing had been left unpacked except the clothes she would be wearing that evening.

Even the prospect of being in Adam's company didn't fill her with the usual excitement. For a time she wondered if she could get out of going to the celebration by feigning a headache, but Tobias had done nothing to offend her and the celebration was to mark his retirement.

She showered and dressed with her usual care, although her heart wasn't in it, and there was an underlying sense of impatience in her mind. The knowledge that her holiday had been wasted was irritating. She had done what she could to help Alex, but there was a limit to what a friend should expect.

Leaning back, before the dressing-table where she was sitting, she studied her appearance in the mirror. She didn't care if she made a good impression or not. Alex certainly wouldn't notice how she looked and Adam had no further interest now that she was no longer going to marry his brother.

It was no use moping over what might have been, she thought. When she got back to London, winter notwithstanding, she was going to have a good time to make up for this poor excuse of a holiday.

A tap at the door had her turning in her seat, frowning, when Adam looked in at her.

'Are you ready? It's time to leave.' His tone was carefully non-committal, his face set impassively.

She rose to her feet and picked up her handbag, conscious of his gaze. They descended the stairs together, and Cassie keenly felt the tension that seemed to exist between them.

Tobias was standing in the hall and his presence alleviated the awkwardness that had developed.

'Hello,' Tobias said cheerfully. 'You look a picture, Cassie. Did Adam compliment you on your appearance?'

'He did not,' she replied. 'I suspect that he has other things on his mind right now.'

Adam made no comment, and it was Tobias who held her arm as they left the house. The car was waiting, and Adam slid into the driving seat. Tobias ushered Cassie into the back, where they sat together.

'I booked a table at the Trade Wind restaurant,' Tobias said when Adam was driving them to town. 'Afterwards we can go on to the night club, if you wish. It has been many a long year since I went out to paint the town red, I can tell you! But if I happen to turn tired halfway through the proceedings then I'll leave you and Adam to enjoy yourselves in my place.'

'You don't have to go to all this trouble, Tobias,' Adam said sharply, his shoulders stiff.

Cassie stared at the back of Adam's head, wishing she dared reach out and touch it. She smiled as the impulse gripped her, but shrugged away the urge. This time tomorrow she would be many miles away and she'd have to forget everything that had happened here and the man she'd fallen in love with.

'Where's Alex?' she asked casually. 'Isn't he coming to this celebration?'

'It seems that he has other things to do,' Adam replied, his tone cool. 'Since he's learned that he has to take his place in the business he's gone over the top, as I expected he would, and at the moment he's making a lot of smoke but no fire.'

'He's enthusiastic,' Tobias said quietly. 'There's no substitute for that, Adam, so don't put him down because of it.'

'I'm all for it,' Adam assured him.

'Don't get me wrong. I hope Alex does prove himself. Then perhaps he can run the business successfully while I go off play-boying around the pleasure-spots of the world.'

'If you really want to get out of harness for a spell, I could remain until you returned,' Tobias offered.

Cassie fancied that she detected hope in his tone. She began to wonder if he really would retire. He had been working for so many years it was probable that he couldn't call a halt.

Adam must have been of similar mind for he chuckled and said, 'If you do leave the island it will be a miracle, Tobias. I won't believe you've retired until after you've actually gone.'

Tobias laughed. 'I know I've threatened to pull out before, but this time I really mean it,' he said.

Cassie had the feeling that the evening would be a very long drawn-out ordeal, but when they entered the restaurant the atmosphere seemed to ease.

Adam began chatting to her, and two sherries later she was able to appear light-hearted without too much of an effort.

They had hardly begun the meal when Alex arrived, accompanied by a young woman who could only be Kirsty, Cassie decided, and she felt the tension well up inside her as they approached the table.

'Hello, everyone!' Alex was aggressively cheerful as he pulled out a chair for Kirsty. 'You've met Kirsty before, Tobias. And you know her, Adam. Cassie, meet Kirsty. Kirsty, Cassie.'

'Hello,' Cassie said, and the girl replied somewhat self-consciously.

'I'm pleased to see you, Kirsty,' Tobias said. 'That hasn't always been the case, unfortunately. But that was more your father's fault than anything.' He paused and smiled faintly. 'This is a retirement celebration. After forty-five years, I'm going back to England for the remainder of my days.'

Kirsty opened her mouth to reply but

Adam's face showed displeasure, and he suddenly leaned across the table toward Alex.

'You have no sense of propriety, Alex!' He rapped out the words. 'You could at least wait until Cassie left before being seen out with another girl.'

'You're a stick-in-the-mud, Adam!' Alex retorted, grinning. 'You don't mind that Kirsty is here, do you, Cassie?'

'Not at all,' Cassie replied.

'You were practically jilted by Alex,' Adam protested to Cassie as he leaned back in his seat, 'and I would have expected more of a reaction from you.'

Cassie didn't reply. She glanced at Tobias but he merely shook his head sadly and said nothing.

The next moment, Pierre Marchant approached with Simone at his side. Adam and Alex rose to their feet.

'We're having a little celebration because I am retiring,' Tobias announced. 'Please join us, Pierre. Let's have some more champagne, Adam.'

'Just one drink perhaps,' Pierre responded, frowning as he glanced at Kirsty, then at Cassie. He fetched a chair for Simone, who sat between Adam and Alex, then got one for himself, sitting between Cassie and Tobias.

A waiter arrived and Tobias ordered champagne.

Cassie resumed her interrupted meal.

'Your holiday hasn't ended yet,' Pierre observed to Cassie.

'It has,' she replied. 'I return to London tomorrow.'

'I'm going to England in a few days,' Pierre told her. 'But first I must settle some business with you, Adam. I cannot leave that deal suspended until my return.'

'You'll have to talk to Alex about that now,' Adam informed him, and Cassie glanced at him in surprise. 'With Tobias leaving the business, we are having to reorganise,' Adam continued. 'In future, Alex will be handling any business relating to the island and this side of the Atlantic. I'll brief him on any outstanding deals, but he's the man in charge now.'

'And what will you be doing?' Simone asked, her expression pensive.

Adam smiled. 'Travelling a great deal, I hope. I'm going to take care of our European and Middle Eastern interests. I've been stuck in these parts far too long. In the very near future I'll be visiting our branches abroad and promoting business farther afield.'

'He's going to take over what I've been doing these past few years,' Alex said with a grin. 'It's about time he changed his image. Staying too close to home has made him dull.'

Cassie listened in silence to the chatter and wished again that it had been Adam instead of Alex who'd visited England six months before. If she had met him first there might have been a different ending to her holiday. But now he had big ideas, and would soon find fresh interests and new faces when he began to travel. He had plans for the future and, unfortunately, she didn't figure in them.

She was able to sit unobtrusively while Pierre and Simone were present, but as soon as father and daughter withdrew she was once more drawn into the general conversation. Now business loomed, but Tobias cut in sharply.

'No more shop-talk tonight,' he warned. 'I don't want to hear another word. He glanced at his watch. 'In fact, I think I might have overdone it. I'd better go home. I'm too tired to sit here trying to whoop it up. We've had a nice meal, and that's enough for me.'

'It's early yet,' Alex protested. 'I thought we were going on to the night club.'

'That's strictly for young folks,' Tobias told him regretfully.

'I'd rather not go, thank you,' Cassie said. 'If you're going home, Tobias, then I'll drive you. I'd like an early night. I shall have to be up early in the morning.'

'You should make a real night of it,' Alex said. 'Come with us, Cassie. Adam will make up a foursome.'

Cassie was watching Adam's face to see how he received the suggestion, but he was staring moodily across the restaurant, and she cringed at the thought of spending the rest of the evening in his company when he couldn't conceal his disinterest.

'No, thank you.' She smiled casually, although there was an ache in her heart. 'I'd better have an early night. Let me drive you home, Tobias.'

'I think we should all go home,' Adam stated firmly.

'Something tells me that a wet blanket has been thrown over the proceedings,' Alex observed. 'Well, if that's the case, Kirsty and I will take ourselves off and make our own entertainment. You three staid old people can go home to your hot milk and an early night.'

Tobias arose and prepared to depart. Cassie followed him, walking ahead of

Adam. They returned to the house in near silence, and Cassie's heart was near to breaking as she wished the older man goodnight and went up to her room. All that was left to her now was the counting of the hours left before she boarded her flight to England.

* * *

She soon discovered that sleep couldn't be induced. She lay in silver starlight, the scintillating heavens open to her troubled gaze as she considered going home. Cassie realised now that anything would be better than just departing and slamming the door irrevocably upon what could have proved to be a wonderful future.

She arose and pulled on a dressing-gown, then crossed to the window and stared out into the gleaming shadows. A faint breeze caressed her face, scented by the exotic flowers growing in the garden. The house seemed to oppress her, and she pushed her feet into slippers and left the room quietly to tiptoe down the stairs and out on to the terrace.

She looked up at the house. There was a light in Alex's room, but Adam's window was in darkness.

A window squeaked open and she glanced up quickly. It was Alex's window, and she saw his head appear.

'Is that you, Cassie?' he asked.

'Yes. I couldn't sleep. Thought I'd come out to the garden,' she called back up to him, her voice echoing in the silent darkness.

'I'll come and join you.' His head disappeared from the window.

Cassie sighed as she paced the terrace, feeling like a caged tiger. A few moments later, Alex emerged from the house and approached quietly, his face shadowed.

The moon was not yet above the horizon and starlight alone was deceptive. She looked up at him. He was wearing casual clothes, and for a heart-stopping moment she could imagine that this was

Adam before her.

Alex soon spoiled the illusion by lounging, as was his habit. It came home to her that Adam was more vital in his mannerisms, less casual, and she treasured the thought.

'What's bothering you, Cassie?' He stood at her side. 'Don't you want to go home tomorrow?'

'I don't, and that's the plain truth of it,' she admitted.

'It sounds as if you have a bad case of *Adamitis*!' He chuckled. 'Am I right? Hey, wouldn't it be great if you married Adam and became my sister-in-law? But Adam has been giving you a hard time of it ever since we arrived, hasn't he?'

'He did put me through the wringer,' she admitted, 'although I can see now that he had your best interests at heart, Alex.'

'You're in love with him!' His voice was filled with concern. 'You came all the way out here to fall in love with my twin brother.'

She didn't reply, and he placed a hand on her shoulder.

'Poor Cassie. Is there anything I can do to help? Shall I sound Adam out for you? There's no telling how he feels. He wouldn't reveal any emotion because he's been under the impression that you and I were engaged.'

'I know that only too well!' She clenched her hands. 'And because of that stupid lie you told Tobias I couldn't act naturally in Adam's company. Everything went your way, Alex, while I was stranded high and dry.'

Alex's hand pressed her shoulder and she clasped his wrist.

'You didn't answer my question,' he said. 'Are you in love with Adam?'

She stared across the terrace. In the distance a pair of headlights gleamed, coming steadily nearer, flickering as tree trunks showed between her and the vehicle. She thought the car was being driven too fast, and frowned as she glanced up at Alex.

'Someone's coming,' she observed.

'Did Adam go out again after we came back from town?'

'How would I know? I wasn't here. And I've never bothered myself with Adam's activities.' He shook her gently. 'Will you answer my question?'

'If you weren't so wrapped up in your own little world you'd quite easily see that I'm in love with Adam,' she retorted bitterly. 'But what's the use? I'm going home in the morning.'

The headlights of the approaching car swung and came toward the house.

Cassie watched them with narrowed eyes, her thoughts bitter.

'I love you, Cassie!' The words were a mere whisper in her ear.

She was startled at what he'd just said and she tried to twist round and look up into his face but he held her so tightly, that she couldn't move.

'Alex, what are you saying? What about Kirsty? You couldn't possibly love me. There's never been anything between us. And I couldn't love you after meeting Adam!'

The car pulled in beside the terrace and its door swung open. Adam alighted, slammed the door and came running up the steps to the terrace. At the last moment he spotted them and hesitated, turned toward them, and Cassie's breath caught in her throat.

It wasn't Adam! It was Alex! His movements were unmistakable. She narrowed her eyes to get a better look at his face as he came forward a few paces.

'Cassie? Adam?' he said. 'Oh! Sorry for intruding! I didn't really see you there. Goodnight!' He turned and went swiftly into the house.

Cassie shivered despite the warm glow that suddenly suffused her body. Again she tried to turn but Adam held her motionless.

'Adam! You pretended to be Alex to trick me! You even put on some of Alex's clothes. I remember you saying when I first arrived that you and Alex used to assume each other's identities for days on end to fool people.'

201

He chuckled and spun her around and drew her into his arms. As he kissed her, Cassie's arms slid upwards and encircled his neck.

'I couldn't let you leave without trying to discover the truth,' he told her. 'I sensed that you were in love with me, but you were apparently engaged to Alex. I didn't make a breakthrough until Tobias gave me the truth of it this evening after we came home.

'Alex had told him about Kirsty this afternoon, and explained that you and he were never engaged. When I learned that I began to understand a great deal. I sensed from the start that you and Alex were not in love, and that threw me completely. I thought you were out for what you could get, and I felt guilty when I fell in love with you, believing as I did that Alex was going to marry you.'

'You fell in love with me?' she repeated. 'And are you going to let me go back to England tomorrow?' she asked then.

'No.' He shook his head emphatically.

'Alex had made a plane reservation for you but I cancelled it. That was why I was getting so desperate this evening. I was thoroughly miserable when we went to the restaurant. You seemed so set against me. You wouldn't even go on to the night club because you didn't want to be in my company. That's why I had a showdown with Tobias when we came home.

'I finally realised that something was going on behind the scenes when Alex arrived at the restaurant with Kirsty and Grandfather didn't turn a hair. I threatened to leave the business myself unless Grandfather told me exactly what was going on, and it was only then that he explained.'

Cassie could only stare wordlessly at him, her mind filled with tumultuous joy because she wasn't booked to fly out in the morning.

'This evening was their joint idea,' Adam went on. 'They thought you would be leaving on the morning plane and were afraid that I'd let you go without doing something about us.

'That's why I masqueraded as Alex,' he continued. 'I was desperate to find out what was in your mind, and you told me because you thought I was Alex. I don't think I could have fooled you in daylight, but starlight was made for this little deception.'

He took her into his arms, and, before she could catch her breath, his mouth closed upon hers.

'I love you, Cassie.' His whispered words floated through the perfumed night.

'And I love you, Adam.'

He eased back a fraction and looked down at her, eyes gleaming in the shadows. 'Will you stay on here with me until I can make arrangements to go to Europe?' he asked. 'We can put the misunderstandings of the past behind us, my love.'

She pressed closer to him, her heart thudding with joy. 'I'll stay anywhere with you,' she whispered.

Cassie closed her eyes as Adam

kissed her again, and the doubts of the past two weeks dropped away from her mind. Their hearts beat together in unison, and she realised that was how it would be for the rest of their lives.

THE END

We do hope that you have enjoyed reading this large print book.

Did you know that all of our titles are available for purchase?

We publish a wide range of high quality large print books including:
Romances, Mysteries, Classics
General Fiction
Non Fiction and Westerns

Special interest titles available in large print are:
The Little Oxford Dictionary
Music Book, Song Book
Hymn Book, Service Book

Also available from us courtesy of Oxford University Press:
Young Readers' Dictionary
(large print edition)
Young Readers' Thesaurus
(large print edition)

For further information or a free brochure, please contact us at:
Ulverscroft Large Print Books Ltd.,
The Green, Bradgate Road, Anstey,
Leicester, LE7 7FU, England.
Tel: (00 44) **0116 236 4325**
Fax: (00 44) **0116 234 0205**

THE FAMILY AT FARRSHORE

Kate Blackadder

After breaking up with Daniel, archaeologist Cathryn Fenton quite happily travels to Farrshore in Scotland to work on a major dig. In the driving rain, she gives a lift to Canadian Magnus Macaskill, then finds that they both lodge at the same place. The dig goes well, with Magnus filming the proceedings for a Viking series. But trouble looms in Farrshore — starting when Magnus learns that his son Tyler is coming over from Canada to be with his dad . . .

THE TEMP AND THE TYCOON

Liz Fielding

Talie Calhoun had briefly met billionaire Jude Radcliffe whilst working as a temp at the Radcliffe Group. It was a rare holiday away from nursing her invalid mother. But when she's asked to accompany Mr Radcliffe to New York, she is over the moon. However, Radcliffe is furious with his secretary's choice of temp. But Talie is a vibrant woman and, as he becomes drawn to her, Jude becomes determined to take care of her and make her his own.

LOVE TRIUMPHANT

Margaret Mounsdon

Steve Baxter disappears while interior designer Lizzie Hilton is working on the refurbishment of his property. His brother, Todd, suspects Lizzie of becoming romantically involved with Steve, knowing that he is due to come into an inheritance upon marriage. Lizzie challenges Todd to find evidence to substantiate his outrageous allegation. But when Paul Owen appears on the scene Lizzie panics — because Paul can provide Todd with the evidence he is looking for . . .

FORGET-ME-NOT

Jasmina Svenne

As girls, Diana Aspley and Alice Simmonds swore that they would be friends forever. So Diana is devastated when she receives the news that Alice has died in unexplained circumstances. Then during her first London Season, she thinks she catches sight of a familiar figure from a carriage window . . . Diana is determined to get to the truth about Alice's fate, even if she has to persuade the aloof and eminently eligible Edgar Godolphin to help her.